Content Page

WARNING!!

This book contains abstruse topics such as Dark Love, Abuse, Violence etc if you are not comfortable with the above please feel free to swipe past this book.

Chapter 1

I looked at the crisp page of the book I held in my hand. Right at the bottom, it read page 108. I sighed, slowly sipping my hot creamy coffee. I have been reading the same page for the past 30 minutes. I had a lot on my mind. You would think after three months of peace, I would not be so jumpy and paranoid anymore. Wrong. Although I had to admit I was now better than before, way better. At least the panic attacks occurred only a few times a week now.

I looked outside the big window of the diner, sighing as my eyes darted all over the place once again for the twelfth time today. Still nothing there. No one there. He's not here. I told myself, averting my eyes from the big window. No matter how many times I would tell myself that, I could only partially believe it. Deep down, I knew better, but I promised myself I wouldn't live like that anymore. I promised myself to actually give myself a chance at life.

Just as I averted my gaze, my eyes looked at a red-haired figure taking orders in the diner with a smile on her face. I looked at my carefree friend as she pulled out her tiny notepad and sweetly spoke to the customers. I would give anything for my life to be that carefree again. I would give anything just to taste the feeling of true peace and not looking over my shoulder. The feeling of not being scared anymore. Oh, how I missed the days spent with my mom in her kitchen singing gospel music while we cooked.

Jane was my friend of two months. I've been in this town for almost three and a half months now, and in that duration, I had made only two friends somehow. I never had a hard time making new friends; it was my situation that forced me to keep my distance. The first month, I had completely isolated myself, which was truly the hardest thing for me to do. I was the kind of person who loved being surrounded by friends and family, not necessarily in a place, but knowing that I had someone always made me happy. So just disappearing and being alone was hard, but I had kept my distance because I didn't want any more people dying in my name anymore.

Even though I have friends, I kept them at arm's length. Afraid they would get hurt if they got too close. Jane was the happiest person I knew, yet she was a single mother of a beautiful little five-year-old boy, and her paycheques from this very diner helped her pay the bills. She was barely making it on her own, but she was always so happy. I adored her. Her mood always rescued me from the thoughts of my terrifying past. Her son was the cutest thing I've ever seen. I've always loved kids; that's why I had studied to be a second-grade teacher. I just wanted to be surrounded by them, and I wanted to be a teacher someday.

Jane's son James adored me. I babysit every time I get the chance because I simply cannot get enough of the little man and because I want my friend to have a break every now and then. Whenever I think about that little boy, my ovaries always scream yes, but my mind, body, soul, bank account, and past say no. My past said no. I knew if I was to ever have a child, it would be his; otherwise, he would kill that child, just like he almost put a bullet through a two-year-old child I was looking after when he thought the baby was mine just after we met.

I shivered at the thought. Don't think of him, don't think of him. I calmly thought to myself I didn't want to have another panic attack. Today was Friday; I was supposed to be at school teaching my little children, but it was a holiday, and my heart honestly hurt at not seeing them. I quietly placed my book on the table, huffing at the two braids that were now covering my face. I had left them to fall freely around my face this morning because it looked cute in the mirror, but now I regretted that decision because they were now annoying and blocking my eyesight at every chance they got.

I untied my braids, making them fall onto my face and shoulders before taking all of them together and placing them in a bun on top of my head. I could honestly care less right now about how I looked; I just wanted to be unbothered. I quietly went back to my reading, not before checking the time, knowing that Jane was about to clock off. She was giving me a ride to my apartment after her shift. I had decided to spend my Friday cooped up in this diner just reading. I've always loved reading, but for the past few months, I wouldn't lie and say I've honestly enjoyed a good book.

I didn't have the same concentration and curiosity that I did. I would start reading off to a good start, and then my mind would start to wander. Was he watching me? Was he coming? Was he purposely making me believe that I successfully escaped him? Thought after thought. And then I would end up drowning in my thoughts; sometimes I would swim way too deep in my thoughts that I would end up having panic attacks. I didn't mind them anymore because they were usually in the walls of my apartment where I would hold myself and sob myself to sleep.

I looked at the people around me in the diner, feeling more than one set of eyes on me. My eyes led me straight back to Jane, who was staring at me. I raised a brow in question before she smiled at me and nodded her head towards Blake before winking at me. Blake didn't fail to notice my gaze because he was already staring at me. He was sitting at a table not so far from mine but far enough with some more familiar faces that I have seen around town before. The man was appealing to the eyes; I wouldn't even lie, but I wouldn't even dare to think of him like that. I knew better.

Jane claims I'm too beautiful to be single if that's even a thing. She's been trying for weeks to get me to go out with Blake. He was the perfect guy in her books. I knew Blake had a thing for me; anyone could see that aside from that he had made that more than obvious to me that he liked me. He makes me think of the life that I had wanted. I would never even think about going out with him no matter how many times he asks. No matter where I hide, no matter where I go. I would never ever in my right mind bat an eye at another man let alone let him take me out. I had scars to prove how things would go if I did. Deep, painful scars.

I looked down at the ring on my ring finger. On my right hand. I felt my heart quicken just by the glimpse of it. His ring. No matter the assurance I would get or have of not crossing paths with him again, I would never take it off. Not because I didn't want to, God knows I wanted to but because I was terrified to. My body would physically tremble whenever I would try. He always kept his promises, and he made sure I knew that there would be consequences if I ever was to take his ring off. I just thank God that he didn't put a tracker on it, her people confirmed it.

Whenever people would ask if I was engaged or anything, I would tell them it was my grandmother's ring and I wore it to feel safe and close to her. I didn't like nor want to talk about my past. After that, they would never bring the topic up ever again. That was what normal people do but not Jane or Aliyah. They would push, but when they felt they were going too far, they would back off. Aliyah was my other friend, a sapphire at heart. She was the more realistic one. I met her through Jane; they were best friends since diapers, and they welcomed me into their little circle.

Aliyah was the one to tell Jane when she was being too out of this world. They were James' parents. Aliyah has never left Jane's side ever since she fell pregnant and the douchebag wanted nothing to do with the child. That had earned him a mean punch from Aliyah before they never heard from him ever again. They both provide for James, and he was really close with both of them. I truly adored their relationship, they were like sisters. A relationship I knew nothing about. They both worked very hard.

Aliyah was one of the best lawyers I've ever seen; I've seen her in court, and she crushed the opposition every time, but she has been struggling for a while now. She just started her own firm, and so far it wasn't going so well, but I knew it was only a matter of time before her firm blossomed. None of my friends had it easy. Jane was also a student in her free time; she was studying business on the side. I truly admired both women. Stronger than ever. And even stronger together. They were both in steady relationships which is why Jane always wanted to see me on a date, but I knew she only wanted what was best for me.

"Ready to go." I quickly looked up startled and calmed down when I saw Jane smiling at me with her bag on her shoulder and her car keys in her hand. I simply gave her a smile back and nodded before standing up. The moment we started walking Jane started rambling on about Blake and I's cute mixed babies making me groan and tune her out.

When we finally made it outside the diner I took a deep breath in, loving the feeling of being outside. I quickly looked around me before we started walking to her car. I wasn't surprised that Jane was still going on about the babies but now she was going on about James marrying my baby if it's a girl and how we all live happily ever after. I truly loved her personality I wish I was this happy. I honestly wished I had a simpler life. A life where I would wake up go to my so-called job, come back to a special someone and hang out with my friends on the weekend. Too bad I had a Powerful Psychotic Man refusing to let me go.

I looked out the window as the car pulled off. Looking at the scenery as the car moved. I almost choked on air when I saw a familiar face staring at me in the diner. Sitting exactly where I was sitting by the big window. Before I could properly look at the man the car zoomed past the diner. It's not him. I simply told myself calming down. There was no way that that was him because if he was here then that meant he was close. I would have known by now if he was close. He could never stay away from me. He never wanted me far from him. This was just my mind playing tricks on me again.

I sighed once again wiping my itchy hands on my dress and paying more attention to Jane as we indulged in one of her deluded topics. Tomorrow was Saturday meaning my nephew was spending the day with me. I could feel myself get happier by the second at the thought of him coming over. I felt happy because I knew that I was a few hours closer to seeing James. I knew I would stay up all night baking him cookies but I didn't mind at all as long as his blue eyes would go big as saucers and his mouth would open in glee. I loved seeing the excitement in his eyes. I loved seeing him happy.

"I will see you tomorrow." I said getting out of her car and closing the door as she crazily waved goodbye with a big smile on her face which made me chuckle and smile genuinely back. I quietly made my way into my apartment taking a quick shower before getting started on my baking. The smell of the cookies made me sigh in content I could honestly get used to this life.

...

Chapter 2

Chapter 3

'The next time you hesitate I will put a bullet through you.' was the last thing I heard. The last thing that rang through my head as my world turned dark.

When I woke up again, I was in bed naked, the blood cleaned free from my legs and bum. The pain was still as unbearable as before. Half of my body was on top of him, my head on his chest with his arm around me. Even though I woke up a while ago and darkness surrounded us it was at night, I knew Sylas was awake. I didn't need to feel or see him move to know that he was awake, I could feel it even with his levelled breathing.

I knew that he felt the hot tears flooding his chest from my sore eyes. I knew that he felt the tremble of my body and the shake of my chest. I silently cried. Not only from the unbearable pain from my bum but because I didn't understand what I did wrong. Was this my life now, just being oblivious to when he would strike again. I did everything his way, I didn't want to end up hurt.

I won't deny considering leaving with his mother; one wouldn't believe how many times I've dreamed and wished for escape. I held my breath when I felt his hand slightly tighten around my waist, just tight enough to restrain me without causing pain. My heart started racing at his slight movement, and I closed my eyes to calm myself.

"I swear I wasn't going to leave with her; I didn't even know she was coming," I whispered, closing my eyes once again. They felt heavy. I feared he wasn't done with me; I blacked out amid his lashes. I feared he would continue where he left off. Living in fear was cruel, something I'd never wish on anyone, not even my enemies.

It felt crucial for Sylas to know I had no part in this because I didn't know what he was thinking. I didn't want to go through what I went through again. I doubted I could handle it. I was so scared of what was going through his head.

"I know," he replied, his voice deep and rough. There was no movement from his body.

"I wasn't going to go with her," I slowly said, wanting him to know. I needed to say it with Sylas; everything could turn bloody in a matter of seconds. The last thing I needed or wanted was him thinking I wanted to go with her, even though that was the case. With everything in me, but I knew I couldn't. He didn't need to know that. It would be better for me if he didn't know my true intentions at that moment.

"You would have never left the gates even if you did choose her," he stated. I had thought about what would have happened if I had picked a different path. Even with everything, I couldn't help but think. Those thoughts and the regret of how I might have had a chance and how I was too much of a coward to take it washed over me. It had been weighing heavily on my mind the moment she walked out the door. Hearing Sylas say that, I felt thankful for choosing to stay with him.

What I didn't understand through all of this was why he hurt me. I did everything he asked. I chose him at the chance of my freedom. I didn't understand what I did to piss him off.

"Sylas, I chose you; I don't understand why you hurt me when I chose you," the lump in my throat grew with every passing second. I wanted to move away from him, but I was too scared to.

"You hesitated," he started, now slowly tracing his fingers over my painful bum. It felt like it was on fire. I didn't understand the last thing he had said to me. I thought he couldn't possibly hurt me because I hesitated. It was human nature; what did he think I would do? I didn't want to be here, so any chance to be away from him would seem admirable to me. I was bound to hesitate. I was fighting two sides of myself, two very convincing sides.

"Do you understand what will happen to you the next time I tell you to do something, and you hesitate?" he asked, his voice deep and low. I wished his mother and I could have somehow made it; at least now I knew she was speaking the truth before. I nodded my head, the lump in my throat too big to speak.

I whimpered, biting my bottom lip as tears rushed down my face when I felt a slap on my already painful butt. I felt like screaming. I knew my bottom lip would be bruised by morning; I felt as if letting it go would make me burst. The pain of his slap lingered as my body froze. He didn't need to speak. I knew why.

"Yes, I understand," I whispered, my body frozen in his arms.

"Good, now sleep," he said. It was easy for him to say, considering the pain I was in. I couldn't believe I had actually dated him, that I had actually felt things for him. He was so cruel. How did I not see? To be fair, Sylas had never truly made me doubt him. Sure, he may have raised a few red flags during our first encounter, but I was drunk, and I thought he just had a tint of dark humour.

After the bar, everything went smoothly. We never got into arguments because most of the time Sylas would say I'm right when I would start arguing over silly things. At first, it worried me how amazing he was with me. I didn't blame myself for worrying; there were a lot of men putting up facades out here, but Sylas was different. I only got to see his angry 'my way or my way' side when it was arguments concerning me and us.

He just didn't seem to care about the silly little arguments. The only time our arguments ever got serious was when he would speak about me moving in and we only argued about it twice, I guess twice was more than enough for him. To be fair he did tell me he wouldn't ask three times and I thought he was joking. I think I was kind of terrible at reading people, actually at reading him.

Either way, that Sylas was an amazing boyfriend well with kinks here and there, for starters he was madly possessive but I kinda liked that side of him, it turned me on... before. I was also possessive but I think Sylas changed the meaning of the word. Clearly he now took that to another level. I don't know what changed, I think he was just always like this but Sylas wasn't one to pretend ever. So I don't understand what happened to the other part of him.

I had strongly went over the idea of him pretending to be that man but it didn't seem right I didn't know what to think anymore. I should have left him when he bought that restaurant for me just because I said I like the golden theme and designs they had, it was a fancy restaurant and we had only been there once. I knew he was intense but I didn't expect that. He was just full of surprises.

At times even when he would look at me I would find myself breathless. In his eyes I felt like I was everything to him, he made me feel that way. That's what he had told me once, I remember not knowing what to say but not freaked out because I had come to learn how blunt and intense he was. There was always a way that he would look at me at times that had butterflies shooting through my stomach and a smile on my face that I couldn't help.

Now, now I doubted it would do the same.

...

There was so much I wanted to say. My chest felt tight, I wanted to scream, cry and hurt him. I quietly watched his muscled back as he headed into the walk-in closet with only a towel around his waist. I was pretending to be asleep I didn't want to talk to nor acknowledge him. It's been three days since the incident and Sylas has been Sylas.

I still didn't understand how he could be like this. It is very hard for me to abandon my teachings and beliefs that there is some good in everyone but Sylas was making me question that everyday. I didn't understand nor believe how a person could be so evil. It didn't make sense to me.

Above every other emotion I felt hurt. Very hurt. My mind felt heavy so did my body. I felt like giving up on everything. Sylas can be so confusing it made my heart hurt. When he looks at me at times, he looks at me like I'm the centre of his world but then when he decides he wants to hurt me his eyes are something else.

"I know you are awake." he said putting on his shirt his muscles flexing on accord. I froze slowly properly opening my eyes as I sat up looking at him no longer peaking at him.

"Why are you so cruel so me?" I started, staring at my hands. I couldn't look at him. Not right now.

"I remember a time when you would do anything for me." I dryly chuckled tears rolling down my cheeks. I remember a time when I would get him to do almost anything for me. Currently that was all I could think about.

The tears came stronger at the memory of our relationship. I remember asking him to try street food, a bratwurst. Of course I had figured the way Sylas carries himself he had never had a taste of street food, at a point I didn't even think that he took walks on the street before me. I liked taking walks and he didn't want me walking around alone without him. I also really enjoyed taking walks with him, at first he was so rigid and stoic but as time went on he became normal-ish. Well as normal Sylas can get.

I could tell most of the times when he did something for the first time with me. I found it cute and intriguing. Some things just looked weird being done by him. His cars, house, suits and just him screamed elegance. It was funny watching his face change when he had the first bite. I couldn't even be that mad at him when he threw it away and mine in the process. It was quite funny as he spoke about my health and continued lecturing me on taking care of myself. He did make it up to me.

I couldn't help but chuckle at the memory. I could never truly stay mad at him for long. Ironically I kind of missed those days.

"I remember a time when my smile meant something to you. When my happiness meant something to you. I don't think you have ever lied to me but I'm starting to question that." his stare didn't stagger as he put on his suit jacket before sliding his hands into his pockets. I looked at him, really looked at him. I felt so vulnerable but I didn't care I had a feeling we had a life time together and I had no say in that.

"You haven't smiled or laughed in five days. I notice and see everything about you. When you are obsessed with something it tends to over power every other thought in your mind." he said tying his tie, his focus on me. He caught me off guard.

"I don't like seeing you cry or sad but if you keep on playing with your life, I might just end up taking it." he said not moving an inch, his eyes darker.

"I've never lied to you, remember when I told you that your smile is breathtaking?"

"Yes." I didn't recognise my own voice at this moment.

"I wasn't lying. Everything about you to me is perfect. The first time you smiled at me at that restaurant while drinking irresponsibly alone with all kinds of people around you. Your smile is the reason I didn't drag you out of there screaming and kicking. I wanted to try and be normal for you. Your innocence was baffling and angering at the same time."

"Why did you want to drag me out?" I asked needing him to elaborate. That seemed to be one of the things he said I was stuck on.

"You were heavily drinking alone putting your life in danger. You don't know the kind of crazy people surrounding you yet you had the audacity to let your guard down putting yourself in danger." he said. I looked at him for a second before I started chuckling with tears trailing down my eyes.

"B-but you were the monster."

"I know. Exactly my point." he said coming closer. I couldn't help but chuckle in disbelief even though he looked serious.

"Sylas." I started. He didn't answer, he just raised a brow looking at me as if telling me to go on.

"I don't mean to offend you in anyway b-but do you maybe sometimes hear voices in your head?-"

"-It's nothing to be ashamed of, all of us are special in different ways."

"Yes." he said. When I asked the question I didn't know what to expect but his answer had my skin crawling.

"Y-yes. Oh- okay that's- that's.. Uhm. Okay- what do they say, the voices. What do the voices say?" my palms were sweaty as I continuously rubbed them on my thighs.

"A lot, sometimes we disagree with each other but most of the time we agree."

"D-disagree like w-what?"

"The first night I met you. I wanted to do more than just cut-"

"Sylas."

"Yes Mäuschen."

"You are scaring me." I whispered.

"You asked." he said a confused expression taking over his features.

"I-I know but I-"

"Are you disturbed by what I am telling you Mäuschen?" he lightly asked as if a chuckle would follow but it never did.

"I- no-"

"Do you want to know what they are telling me now?" he asked taking a step closer his hands still in his pockets, instinctively I moved back a bit. I couldn't help it.

"No- what?"

"Come here and I will show you." he said.

"I-I didn't-" I couldn't help the fear drenching over me.

"Should I come get you?" he asked raising a brow. I wiped away my tears with my trembling hands looking at him.

"I'm sorry." I whispered I didn't know what for but I just prayed he would forgive me.

"I just wanted to kiss you. Why are you crying?"

"I-I'm scared."

"I just wanted to kiss my naive woman, why are you scared?" he asked chuckling. I paused looking at him before taking a pillow next to me without thinking and throwing it at him.

"That's not funny!" I exclaimed tears halfway down my face. His deep laughter was soothing me in a way it shouldn't have been, it's been a while since I've heard it. This man was sick. He easily ducked the pillow before raising a brow at me, his laughter dying down.

"Sorry." I whispered. Going back to my nervous state.

"Mäuschen why would you think I hear voices in my head."

"Because- you are- you just concern me a lot at times." I was so happy I managed to clean up that sentence.

"Is this because I kill people?" he asked as if it was the most normal thing ever. I- sniffed pausing for a second. How did he expect me to answer this.

"Wwhhha-...N- yes, maybe. Just maybe a little...- yes." I said shrinking away at his eyes.

"Come here. And stop crying." he commanded walking closer to the bed, I didn't hesitate. I didn't want to go through what I went through before. I held my breath when his hand came in contact with my cheek before kissing me. He then moved back looking at me, a look I couldn't decipher glowing in his eyes. Even though I didn't know what it was, it sent a chill down my spine. I didn't miss how he dropped our previous conversation.

"All mine." he whispered in his native tongue. I almost didn't catch it.

"Mäuschen I have no voices in my head telling me what to do, I take my own decisions no one is forcing me to do anything." he said. I weirdly wished he had voices because then maybe I could have convinced myself that it's not him it's the

100

voices but now I know it's all him. I felt more troubled than I did when I thought he heard voices in his head.

"Sylas that wasn't funny. You have a terrible sense of humour." I said looking at him. He had a playful glint in his eyes that looked so foreign in his eyes.

"That's what you wanted to hear. Your innocence strongly amuses me." he said genuinely smiling. As much as he was the devil he was still the most beautiful monster creature I have ever seen. I paused for a second before recollecting my thoughts.

"What do you expect, the last time when you said you killed people for fun, I thought you were joking but look where we are."

"I wasn't joking about that. I was being honest. I would never lie to you." he said coming closer and before I knew it I was swooped up in his arms, my legs around him as he carried me in his arms as if I weighed nothing. I couldn't look away from hypnotising eyes.

"I believe you still need maybe a little help." I softly said placing my hands around his neck, making him chuckle.

"You are all I need." he said his voice deep and husky. I closed my eyes taking in his scent that made me unable to breathe a few days ago.

Before I knew it his lips were against mine

yet again and the kiss was getting heated as he tightened his hands around me. I couldn't take all of him right now, my butt still hurt and I don't think I would be able to survive even a round with him.

"Where would you like to go today?" he said pulling back. I panted looking at him and calming my nerves.

"Don't you have work?"

"Work can wait, where will it be?" I looked at him skeptically. I haven't seen this side of him in a while and I didn't want it to fool me in anyway.

"Maybe we could do some skating." I whispered looking away from him, for some reason I felt he would say no and I didn't want to look at him when his eyes were like this.

"Let's go." he said making me look up at him with my brows furrowed. I didn't understand, neither did I like him acting like this. I low-key wanted him to continue being a jerk because if he went back to his old self I felt it would be too hard for me. I hated being reminded our old memories. I just wanted myself to accept that that was all dead.

If Sylas wanted to be charming he could be very charming and if he wanted to be the devil, he could very much be the devil. Whatever he puts his mind to, he out does himself in every way. I by all means wanted to take a break from this house but I didn't necessarily want to go with. I had a bad feeling about this in my gut.

I looked at Sylas as we entered the building, he effortlessly stood out not only because of his looks or suits but because of the aura he carried with him. He was in one of his casual suits, even though there were a lot of people he didn't have to push or touch anyone, people instinctively moved out of the way as he passed with me beside him. I wasn't even surprised there was just something about him.

Even though his face was emotionless and void of any emotion I could tell that he didn't want to be surrounded by all these people, I wouldn't say uncomfortable but he would rather be anywhere but here, no one else would be able to tell but I could. He didn't like being around a lot of people. He also hated when people touched him. I came to learn that when some girls became too thirsty, it didn't end well. He liked his space. From the first time I met him I now realised a lot of things that I didn't back then.

The building was packed. The place hasn't changed a bit, I noticed as I looked around. The last time I was in here I was with Kutcher we usually came here together, this was one of our favourite spots. I didn't want to take Sylas here because this place was special to me but I needed to feel a bit of familiarity. I needed to feel calm and be somewhere I would be happy and carefree.

Just the thought of Kutcher broke my heart. I stopped texting him and I completely blocked him. After what happened I couldn't even look at or touch my phone without quivering. I knew blocking him would come back and bite me in the ass but at the thought of Sylas I didn't care because pissing of Sylas was far worse than being bit in the ass. Far far worse.

Kill, kill myself or survive. In my head of course I was this badass person who would easily put a bullet through Sylas' head... Sometimes. I cringed at the image. I hated that I wasn't that type of person. I hated that I didn't have it in me to murder someone, anyone for that matter. Kill was definitely out.

Kill myself. Definitely tempting, so so tempting. But I wouldn't do it, not that I couldn't... At least I don't think I couldn't. I wouldn't. I would never do that to myself. I still remember the kid from my high-school who took his life. I didn't know him very well, we had only been having English together but I was devastated, I couldn't help but feel guilty I felt I partly contributed by not noticing. My friend at the time brutally had told me how stupid of a thought that was but that didn't help.

I felt like I could have done something, I felt so sad that something actually drove someone to take their own life. His parents became shells of who they were and so did his friends. It had come as a shock to everyone because he was always so happy and bubbly no one would have ever guessed he was depressed, but it's always the ones you least expect. I never got over it, till this day I wish I could have done something. So taking my own life was out.

Survive. When I had come to terms with this, this option was the only one left. I didn't like it. I don't know why I just didn't like it. Surviving should be so tempting to me. I had too many questions. Does Survival mean, I do what he wants, does it mean I act normal but turn myself into a zombie, does it mean find another way. I haven't figured it out yet. I turned my head and caught him already staring at me.

I forced a nervous smile and closed my eyes as he bent down placing a kiss on my lips. I was overwhelmed and I didn't like being overwhelmed. This wasn't the good or the bad kind of overwhelmed, I was just confused. I sat down putting on my skates. I was a little cold but I didn't want Sylas to know because there was a fifty percent chance that he would make the rash decision of just taking me out of here. I tried convincing him to come on the ice and skate with me but he didn't budge, he had recently got up and walked away claiming he would be back. I didn't care to ask or protest, I would welcome the alone time.

Before I knew it everyone was leaving, I didn't have to ask to know that Sylas was behind this. Apparently they were closing.

We were the only ones left.

"You didn't have to chase everyone out." I said tightening the high boot's laces.

"I know."

"Are you sure you don't want to come with me?" I asked standing up looking at him.

"I'd rather watch, the view is breathtaking from here. " he said taking a seat on the bench, staring at me a glint in his eyes. The glint in his eyes made words hard to pronounce. I turned around before heading on the ice. I hated how he would do that. Have the power to make my words disappear.

As I skated I couldn't help the smile that took over my features, everything felt normal, calm. It has been a while since I've had this feeling. I did a few tricks that Kutcher and I picked up, wanting to see if I still had it after all it has been a while. I chuckled looking around while skating. I remember the first time Kutcher and I came here. He fell on his ass, got up and walked out. I couldn't stop laughing. He waited for me outside and vowed to never come back. He came back. It was always hard for him to say no to me.

I stopped when I realised I was laughing alone when I heard my own small laugh. For a second I thought about how many people I might have freaked out but then I remembered that Sylas chased them away. Sylas. He was the last person I should worry about thinking I've lost my mind but I still couldn't help but look at him.

I glanced at him before I slowed down for a second watching him, a rare smile on his face. It felt abnormal even though it wasn't to me before, I used to stare at it, I still do. I used to love that smile and look forward to see more of it. A warm feeling spread all over my body before butterflies erupted in my stomach when he smiled. He never hid that he loved that he had that kind of effect on me. Sylas wasn't a smiley person but when he did smile, time seemed to always slow down even I had to admit that.

He just sat there on the bench, I've never seen anyone so beautiful in my entire life neither have I ever come across someone so evil. His hard lean body wrapped in one of his suits, grey this time around. It emphasised his eyes. My eyes trailed from his built body to that sharp jawline of his. I wanted to stop right then and there but I couldn't, I looked at his plump naturally pink lips then to his straight nose. I couldn't help the sudden difficulty in breathing when I came to his eyes that never left mine. His eyes felt electric.

I looked away realising I had completely stopped skating. He could always do that to me. At times like these it felt like he could stop time. His blonde hair that was always neatly cut on my mind, even though I didn't spend much time on it I knew exactly how it was. I had spent a lot of my time running my hands through it and just playing with it if he wasn't to edgy. I liked touching him even though he didn't like being touched he didn't seem to mind when I touched him though.

"Come skate with me." I said turning around. I knew he would never and it wasn't his thing and probably never will be. I didn't even push because Sylas has tried almost everything I asked of him and I knew I wouldn't have the slightest of luck when it came to skating. I wouldn't say it was hard for him to say no to me because if he didn't agree with something he made that crystal clear but he did rarely say no to me when it came to me asking for something.

I moved towards him at his command. He was now standing. I got to him careful not to hesitate as I took his hand, holding my breath. How could one be so beautiful yet be so evil. He wasn't on the ice but he was close enough. When I got close enough he didn't waste anytime as he kissed me dominating my mouth and mind, taking his time with me in his hands. I was a bit dizzy after pulling away. His scent was all I could smell.

"Is there a reason why you disturbed my session?" I asked my voice wavering because he was too close. I needed to get my mind away from moving back. His hands were now around my waist they felt like they were on fire, my body felt overly sensitive at this moment.

"No I just wanted to kiss you." he said his facial expression serious as he looked at me. I couldn't look at him any longer in his eyes. I gulped looking away from him. His scent now suddenly overwhelming me.

"Are you sure you don't want to come on the ice with me." I asked the third time. I knew he wouldn't change his mind but I had to change the subject, the glint in his eyes said he wanted to do so much more than kiss me. I feared he would take me right here on the bench and I wasn't fully healed. I was so scared of him. I forced a smile looking at him tears pricking my eyes.

"Go enjoy yourself Mäuschen." he said his arms not budging from around me. I wondered how long he would keep me caged in his arms. I was too afraid to pull back so I kept still.

"How long do we have before we have to go home? " I asked my voice coming out as a whisper.

"Take your time." he said before pecking my lips one more time, unexpectedly letting me go. I didn't waste any time as I went back on the ice, I looked up at the ceiling forcing the tears to stay at bay as I continued skating. I still had goosebumps. I skated for a while longer before I started to enjoy myself again. I really like it here. It made me terribly miss Kutcher but other than that I felt so free on this ice as I spun around and just simply kept on moving.

That was how I spent the day. Sylas made me eat in between even though I wasn't hungry I was too high of the euphoria I felt swooshing through the ice. Someone came in and delivered the food. After eating I went back at it. I felt as if I would never be able to stop and leave because I didn't even feel slightly tired. I told Sylas it was okay if he left and came to get me later but he refused. He just watched me the entire time, I don't even remember him on his phone. I skated until my legs felt sore. They were sore but I felt so satisfied. I finally ran out of juice. I made my way towards Sylas.

"Did you have fun?" he asked.

"Yes, yes I did." I said genuinely.

"Good." he said kissing me.

"Would you like to go home now?" he asked looking down at me as my chest moved up and down.

"Can we come back soon?" I asked hope in my eyes.

"What if I build you your own." he said making me chuckle.

"I know you hate crowded areas with noise but please." I liked being outside every once in a while. He looked at me in his arms for a minute. I had taken of my skates off and fell into his arms. I let him hold me.

"If that's what you want."

I didn't tell him about my sore legs, we exited the building with me in his arms. I was grateful because I didn't want to walk. The last thing I remember is laying my head on his shoulder in the car before I dozed off.

Things seemed like they had gone back to normal. The normal we had when I didn't know about Sylas' urgent need of a mental asylum. Even though I smiled, my mind was still cautious. I haven't forgotten who he is and I don't think I ever will. He was still scary and the fear I had for him could never just disappear. But it was bearable being around him these days.

The past few weeks have been steady. Steady was the right word to Sylas, I honestly didn't know what went on in his mind but to me it was steady. He still gave me goosebumps if he would get too close. He has been weirdly normal, he seems to be back to the man I fell for. Seems. I didn't care though because my mind couldn't shake what he did to me and that look in his eyes when he was mad.

I looked at the smoke coming from the kitchen, I froze and my brows furrowed. Shit. I completely forgot about the pot. I was just taking a mini break, I was really tired from the steaming long morning session with Sylas. Even when I was mad at him, scared of him. No matter the mood. Sylas made it clear that my body belonged to him. He could touch, kiss and do whatever he pleased with me when he wanted to.

I think it was unhealthy how much we had sex. Sylas seemed to differ, he laughed when I had told him this while his hand was around my throat as he railed into me this morning. He never fails to leave me worn out and high of pleasure. Yet no matter how many times he brings me to oblivion over and over and over again I was still scared of him. I was scared of him most when he was quiet that's why I preferred talking to him and him talking to me. Nothing good has ever come from his silence.

I could swear I only sat down for a minute. My mind always seemed to wonder. I stood up from the small bar chair in the kitchen heading over to the stove. There was literally fire in the pot, I've never seen anything like this before it's usually smoke my mind completely shut down I was freaking out because there was fire and because I might burn Sylas' kitchen down. He will kill me.

I quickly poured water into the pot causing a lot of smoke to cover the kitchen. I didn't even have time to do anything else as I was yanked up and pulled out from the smoke. It was so thick in the kitchen one could barely see anything. I couldn't stop coughing as I was placed down in the living room. Sylas. He looked mad. He quietly analysed my body as if looking for something.

"Are you hurt?" he questioned. His face emotionless as he pulled my chin up making me look at him as he analysed my face. I was guessing he just got back from work.

"No." I whispered, my heart was speeding. I watched him look around his smoke filled kitchen.

"Sorry about your kitchen." I whispered looking at his chest. The silence from him was killing me.

"I was just trying to make this new dish for us." I watched in surprise as he now looked into my eyes, he now looked less murder-y.

"Another one of your experiments?" he asked.

"Yes- I'm really sorry about your kitchen." I said yet again as I looked at his kitchen, the smoke was now almost gone.

"I don't care about that. I just don't want you to hurt yourself." he said seriously.

"I didn't hurt myself. I promise." I said softly looking at him.

"Just burn our kitchen down if you please as long as it makes you happy." he gruffly said his voice deep and strong while he snaked his hands around me, kissing my forehead.

"I don't know what happened, I was busy with wait- are you implying that I'm a horrible cook Sylas?" I said raising a brow at him. For the first time in my entire life Sylas looked unprepared. His whole face changed as he looked at me clearing his throat. It was comical but I was still slightly offended.

"I didn't say that Mäuschen. I would never say that I know how much you love experimenting." he said bringing me closer.

"That's not an answer." I said.

"I love your cooking." he said before kissing me.

"Well I'm glad you said that- because as I said before I was experimenting again. I made these-..." I looked at the golden ball shaped things on the kitchen table not far from us as I was still pressed against his chest.

"-Things. Have a taste." I said managing to slip out of his grasp and headed to the kitchen, I took one and held one up to his mouth waiting for him to take a bite. The kitchen was now clear of all the previous smoke.

"Mäuschen you don't even know what they are called." he said skeptically.

"You don't want it?" I asked softly looking at him. I watched him look at me than at it before taking a bite. I smiled satisfied. I couldn't help the warm feeling taking over my stomach as I watched him chew. He kept a straight face.

"They are amazing   ." he said swallowing it. I beamed at him.

"Thank you." I said before taking a bite myself. I coughed hardly swallowing it because I didn't want to spit it out. Oh my God. I think I might one day give myself food poisoning. I looked at him incredulously how on earth did he eat this.

"If you keep on eating my experiments you might end up dead. I don't think this is food." I said sighing while pacing it back on the plate. I didn't understand where I went wrong. He quickly grabbed my waist bringing me close to him.

"They are not that bad." he said his deep voice holding me captive, as he smiled down at me with his perfect face and perfect teeth. I had to take a minute, I didn't like that I had to but I had to.

"You are just saying that." I said breathlessly finding my voice after he stopped.

"This time I didn't almost break my teeth, it's very tasty." he said chuckling.

"You will get food poisoning."

"I don't care." he said making me feel so much better.

"Thank you."

"But no more experiments for now just rest, if you want something ask the chef." he said making me nod my head, before saying yes.

"Please tell me you won't make me stop using the kitchen for my experiments." I asked after a pause my heart sore at the thought. Sylas could easily turn for now to forever if he wanted to.

"No. And if you burn it down because I know you are eventually going to burn it down I will just buy you another kitchen." I smiled in response.

"Thank you." I said feeling relief flush my system.

"As long as you promise to put your safety first because if you hurt yourself then we will have a problem." he said seriously making me shudder. His eyes were now dark and stern.

"Okay." I said nodding. I felt like I was about to take a step from him which would be bad for me, I looked at the kitchen in glee when a thought crossed my mind.

"Oh, I almost forgot I made something else it's in the oven and don't worry the oven is off. It was the first thing I made and-"

Before I could say anything he easily popped the buttons of his shirt open that I was wearing with some shorts, taking my nipple into his mouth. My words got stuck in my mouth as I shivered in his hands. I whimpered when he quickly pulled me up making me wrap my legs around him.

"Sy-Sylas no- this-" I stopped moaning when his teeth pulled my nipple making me arch my back with my eyes closed. I could feel that we were moving but I didn't know where we were going.

My mind was at ease knowing that there was no one in the house it was just the two of us. The shirt I had on had quickly disappeared my bare breasts on display for him as he entertained them with his mouth. Pulling, sucking and licking my hard nipples. The heat coming from in between my legs was unbearable. I could feel his awoken member against me. It was driving me crazy.

I quickly popped my eyes open at the sound of something hitting the ground before my back hit a strong smooth surface. Dinning table. Meaning Sylas just pushed everything on it to the floor. My vase. One of the few things I requested be brought from my apartment. I had moved it here not long ago needing every surface close to me to cool down my things.

"Sylas. You just smashed my vase!" I croaked out, knowing from the sound it was broken, I couldn't see it from the floor as I looked at Sylas who now had only his vest on, his shirt and suit jacket gone. My eyes trailed to his well defined muscles, the vest emphasised his mouth dropping physic. I didn't even realise that my shorts were off until I felt some air against my thighs. My chest was moving up and down as I watched him in frustration a pool between my legs.

"I will buy you another one." he said as he stood between my legs one of his hands behind my neck bringing me closer to him and the other rubbing my pussy through my panties.

"Mmmmmmh." was the only thing I could say as his fingers rubbed circles on my clit that was covered by my now irritating underwear. The water fall between my legs only grew as Sylas' mouth moved from my mouth to my hard nipples. His tongue and teeth made me shiver. I held onto the edge of the table when I felt him slowly take off my panties. I couldn't look at him because of how wet I was.

I gasped when I felt two fingers in me. His thrusts deep and slow before he picked up his pace. I arched my back tightening the hold I had on the table as I came undone with his fingers. I winced when he slowly rubbed my clit, I was still coming down from the high. I squirmed my legs wide open for him placed on either side of the table. He stood in between them, as he rubbed tantalising circles around my clit.

I trembled when I felt his manhood against my core. I held my breath when I felt him slide it in, I could never get used to this. As if possible I tightened my hold against the table knowing what was to come. Sylas didn't give me a moment to catch my breath as he drilled into me. I was a moaning mess. He fucked me through my climax, he didn't give me a chance to breathe as he continued fucking me, his hold strong against my thighs. I climaxed biting my lip in ecstasy.

"Bend over." he commanded. I faltered at his command remembering what happened the last time he bent me over this table. I gulped as I slowly stood making him raise a brow at me. Tired of my sluggish movements he turned me around and roughly slammed me against the table making me tremble in his arms as he parted my legs with his hand, his other hand holding me down. My heart was racing. My nails scratched the bottom edges of the table I was clutching onto for my life as he plunged into me.

I couldn't breathe through my nose as his thrusts became more powerful and deep. I was hardly breathing through my mouth. An orgasm snuck up on me making my eyes tear because of how powerful it was. It left me drained yet Sylas didn't stop. My nails scratched the table when I felt the tightening of my stomach again, I could feel him in my stomach. My legs shook, I came undone holding onto the table as my world seemed to turn upside down.

I was a panting mess when Sylas pulled me from the table lifting me up making me sit on it with my legs wide open for him. The feeling of his body heat and scent so close to me drove me crazy as I tried to register my surroundings.

"I-" his manhood slowly entered me as he tightened his hold against my ass, his mouth on my neck sucking and nibbling away. My eyes were still tightly shut while I panted waiting for his whole manhood to be inside me. It felt like forever. He only gave me a second to adjust to him before he went back to his powerful deep thrusts that left me panting and powerless in his arms. My arms wrapped around his neck when I felt him pick me up before slamming me back down pushing my upper half flat against table. Yet again at his mercy.

I came feeling the orgasm from the tip of my toes to my head, my pussy squeezing his manhood. The throaty raspy fuck he released from his throat as he paused tightening his hold on my thighs made my head spin. It was a second before he went back to thrusting. My eyes rolled to the back of my head on their own accord when I felt him repeatedly hit my g-spot. I trembled releasing a heavy moan that took all of my energy becoming undone yet again, I felt him pause as he shoot his ropes of seed deep inside me. I panted thinking it was over. I was exhausted.

"I want your ass in the air." his deep voice cut through the silence making me shudder. I've had enough yet I wanted more. I should have know better, deep down I knew better but what can I say a girl could dream even with my unmade up mind.

...

I woke up with Sylas coming out of the shower. He told me he would meet me downstairs after I was done with everything. I had thought about just ignoring him and turning in. I was so tired. My body felt beyond tired but I knew he wasn't giving me much of a choice. I don't understand why he wouldn't let me sleep in today. To be fair it was now dark outside but I didn't really care, I was still tired.

Before I got out of bed I opened the draw next to me pulling out the phone that I had completely abandoned. Today was Kellita's birthday. My brows furrowed when I saw 47 missed calls from an unsaved number. I wanted to call it back but I didn't have that kind of time right now neither did I really want to do it. I quickly shot Kellita a text wishing her a happy birthday before taking myself to the shower. I wanted to wish her early this morning but I was knocked out.

After my hot bath, Sylas would have to understand I couldn't stand for a long period of time. I should have soaked my body yesterday like I usually always do after Sylas fucks me until I can hardly remember how to breathe but I didn't really have any time yesterday plus I would have just ended up sleeping in the bath tub, I was so tired. Sylas was an animal because after everything he still had the strength to carry me upstairs, hold me in the shower and help me bathe myself.

I looked at the time on the small clock on the stand, I made it. I surprisingly made it. I made my way downstairs, today I felt needy and really clingy which was also something I bet Sylas already knew. I walked outside to the secluded beautiful place with a big fireplace, dinner was getting laid out in place. I huffed walking out but quickly stopped in my tracks when I was met with a pair of blue eyes. My breath hitched and I almost fell. My gaze fell on an unbothered Sylas.

I took a deep breath before I made my way to him sitting beside him but not before planting a kiss on his lips. My body was already covered with goosebumps when he smiled at me and asked me how I slept. He brought my chair closer to his, he knew how clingy and needy I got after sex. Words seemed to flow out of my mouth but I didn't know what I was saying as I tried to control my emotions. I didn't want to be a part of this anymore, the glint in his eyes was warning enough.

I turned my gaze to his mother who sat not far from us. Tonight we would dine on the small table, I say small because compared to the other one it was a bit small but it was still big enough. For obvious reasons. We left the table in pretty bad shame. Plus the things that Sylas did to me on that table were unspeakable. I remember telling him to burn the table when he carried me upstairs, his response was a chuckle. Plus my scratch marks were all over that table. I liked eating out here though, it was a breath of fresh air.

"Good evening Mrs Harman." I said looking at her a hesitant smile on my face. She smiled greeting me back without missing a heartbeat. A genuine smile on her face.

The dinner was filled with light chatter between his mother and I that I personally tried to keep up with. I made sure to keep my hand on Sylas' hand throughout the dinner, I was afraid of his thoughts. I was more than happy when the dinner came to an end. I understood that she was trying to help me and I was grateful but she should also know that her son was not a force to be reckoned with.

"Would you like to stay and discuss a few things with my mother?" Sylas asked looking at me as he stood up. Not a trace of emotion on his face.

"That would be actually nice. We have a lot to discuss." his mother said looking at me. His mother didn't give a fuck but neither did Sylas and I didn't want to be in between this. On this table I was the only one who actually gave a flying fuck.

"You can stay. I will be in my office." he said standing. I quickly stood up looking at him.

"I want to come with you." I whispered my breath wavering as I clutched onto his hand. I didn't look at his mother at all. I honestly didn't want to end up dead.

Sylas and his mother didn't seem to have anything against each other through out this dinner. They seemed normal with each other, I wished his mother a good night genuinely smiling at her and apologising about having to leave early before I followed Sylas inside. I zoned out for a minute letting him lead the way.

"Mäuschen I need to catch up on something in my office, I will find you in our room shortly." he said when we were at the top of the stairs as he kissed my forehead. I did exactly that. I walked in quickly slipping on one of his shirts and getting in bed. I held his pillow to my chest practically cuddling it, I couldn't help it.

After laying in bed for a minute my mind and heart racing. I concluded nothing peaceful or nice would come out of this. I turned facing my side, I didn't want to think about all this. I opened the drawer on my side getting out my phone, I wanted to call my friend and properly wish her a happy birthday plus I needed to rid my mind of these thoughts.

Before I could dial her number I noticed I had an unread message. I tapped on the notification waiting for a message from Kellita. I froze reading the message over and over again. I could feel my insides turning. I was now in a very tight spot. I was scared of texting back and I was also scared of not texting back knowing the consequences of each action. I felt like crying.

Imagine my surprise when I get to your dad's cabin to find it empty. Haile don't get mad at me the next time we meet, I promised not to do this again but you have left me no choice. I haven't heard from you in weeks and you blocked my number from your phone. You have a lot of explaining to do, I will see you in a few.

Kutcher.

I could feel tears pricking the back of my eyes. I couldn't have Kutcher here Sylas would kill him. I had no doubt in that. I also couldn't text him back and warn him not to come Sylas made it clear that I should stop. I was caught in a cross fire. I closed my eyes trying to control my breathing. I already had enough problems knowing no good would come from Sylas' mother here. And now this. My mind was blank no option seemed to leave me standing. Although I knew I would have to make a decision and I had to make one fast.

I couldn't help the smile on my face as I washed the peeled potatoes. It's been a while since I've woken up happy, today was one of those days. I woke up happy and at peace. I didn't know where the happiness came from, that was a mystery to me but the peace I understood. Sylas' mother left yesterday and that's probably why my insides felt at peace and everything else seemed to be handled. Ever since she was last here when the air between us was sour which was weeks ago, she has made her every now and then visits permanent.

I knew she just came for me, I was grateful but also scared. What always kept me at the edge was the fact that Sylas didn't even seem a bit worried. It was like the whole scene with his mother didn't happen. Sylas would even leave for the whole day while she was here for work and come back late. This time around I miserably failed at trying to read him.

I was scared of speaking to his mother but I did speak to her every now and then because even though there was no escape or hope for me she was trying. I never even once spoke to his mother about anything that would make Sylas cut my legs off. She never once did bring it up when we were alone she seemed like a cunning woman. I concluded the family was crazy because there was no tension whatsoever between Sylas and his mom.

They both spoke to each without any form of bitter emotion. Although she would sometimes remind his son that he didn't deserve me and Sylas would reply with 'I know.' completely unbothered, no tension whatsoever between them while I on the other hand would be holding my breath in my seat. I hated to admit it but it was probably best if his mother stayed away. The feeling that I thought I would at least have of being safe from Sylas' madness while she came to visit was non existent. It was clear that Sylas didn't give a flying fuck.

I didn't understand the dynamic of his mind. He didn't seem to understand my situation. He still takes me out to dinner and whenever he would leave for the whole day for work, he usually worked from home from his office but when he would leave he would always come back with flowers for me. I hated that I secretly liked it not only that but I had started my own guessing game on which type of flowers I would get next.

He does the same thing when he traveled out of the country for a business trip. He rarely traveled out of the country but if he was to, he never came back empty handed, only this time it was far from flowers. I noticed he didn't like taking me with him if it was work related he preferred if I stayed behind. But I especially loved the flowers. I have even started my own little garden. It kept me calm and gave me a sense of serenity.

I felt his stare on me as I looked up at him. He had no shame in getting caught staring in fact he continued as if I didn't just catch him staring at me.

"Aren't you suppose to be slicing some tomatoes?" I questioned averting my eyes.

"I'm done." I looked at the sliced tomatoes in front of him. I wondered how long I was out because he was now done with everything and why didn't he just pull me out of my day dream.

Today I was going to cook but Sylas insisted we do it together. Deep down I knew I was a some what not amazing cook, it depended on what I was making so I wouldn't put myself up there but what I liked and what amused me is the fact that Sylas would never tell me that no matter how shitty my food was. Sylas never lied but when it came to my food all bets were off. I smiled at the thought.

I didn't answer Kutcher's text I blocked him with hopes that when he does locate me he would take the wise decision of backing off after knowing exactly who owns the estate. But of course to my luck nothing ever seemed to go the easy way. Kutcher didn't make it easy for me. He didn't give up. I feared at the rate he was going Sylas would find out and get the wrong idea.

Three days ago he texted me and told me he was outside Sylas' estate. I swear I felt my heart stop for a second. We reached a bargain. I first told him Sylas and I were in love. I tried to be convincing but he didn't seem to buy it I asked him to give me time and in time I would tell him everything. I did also tell him that I couldn't speak to him nor text him any longer over the phone. At first he didn't even want to hear me out but he then reluctantly agreed at last after much convincing and the promise of texting after three days. I made sure to delete every call, text and message.

It's been five days since I've last texted him, Sylas has been around me a lot and I didn't want to risk it. I was too scared to. My body physically couldn't do it when he was anywhere near me. I loved and enjoyed the peace between us and I didn't want anything to trigger his psychotic side. I liked to actually go back to feeling calm around him. I could never really let my guard down around him, the darkness that surrounded him denied me of that but I was better than before.

I watched him effortlessly move around the kitchen, the aroma that filled the kitchen had my mouth watering. Sylas had made me sit down after I knocked over the pot. It was amazing how gentle he could be at times when he pleased. I had sombrely retired to my seat but my mood quickly picked up as I watched him. Even with the relaxed look on his face as he concentrated on his cooking, anyone could feel the dark aura radiating off him. As much as it was scary it also lured you in.

I was surprised by how calmly I was handling the Kutcher situation I didn't panic, I might have almost fainted when he told me he was outside but after that I did everything quietly and quickly. I made sure I didn't make any mistakes. Everything seemed to be in order for now because Kutcher was getting impatient it has been weeks and I liked basking in this side of Sylas. There was no escape so I preferred this side.

"What's on your mind?" he questioned one of his hands in his pockets and the other carried his scotch as he looked at me. My eyes trailed down his body before they went back to his eyes, I couldn't help it. You would never catch the man out of a suit even at home but damn did he make it work. I especially loved it when he wore his shirt with the top buttons popped open, his sleeves rolled up his arms. I felt my face get hot when he raised a brow at me.

"Sylas remember our second date... Well first." I trailed off.

"Second."

"You don't even know which one I'm talking about."

"When I took you to your restaurant." for a minute I even forgot that I had a whole restaurant. I sheepishly smiled at him because he was right, I wasn't surprised.

"Well... Yes. You were so awkward it was actually cute in a dark way."

"Awkward in what way?" he asked picking up his drink as he closed the pot and leaned against the counter looking at me. Till this day he still made me nervous. I didn't understand how one could look so handsome.

"You were so silent in the majority of the date, luckily for you I talk too much when I'm nervous." I said, he chuckled. The chuckle rasp and deep. I had to clear my throat. Evil has never looked so good.

"You call my silence awkwardness?" he asked his accent making it sound foreign.

"Yes. Actually I had accepted that you were the low-key awkward type."

"And what do you think now?" he asked. He seemed greatly interested in everything I did. I watched his eyes move with me as I adjusted the straps of my top.

"Psychopaths are far from awkward Sylas." his throaty laugh filled the kitchen as I watched in a trans. That's something you don't see everyday.

"Why are you silent all the time- why were you so silent that night? Were you judging me?" I asked raising a brow at him remembering that I was actually sober. I watched as he started to elegantly move around the kitchen yet again. Giving the food on the stove his attention and I at the same time.

"No. Everything you did- do greatly piqued

my interest. I didn't understand how to handle such a creature while suppressing the urge that demanded I take you home with me and never let you see the light of day." he said still looking at me his drink now back in his hand. I could hear the rate of my heart pick up.

Well that turned dark very quickly.

Why did he have to be so brutally honest. I fidgeted on my seat as I looked at my glass. The heat of his stare still strong. I wished I had something stronger than water but Sylas would never allow that.

"So you basically consider that our second date-" I paused watching him as amusement flooded his eyes. I disregarded the bar for reasons we both understood.

"-You can't possibly consider the first time you met me as our first date. People were murdered there afterwards and I was kind of drunk. -wait on that note why did you make me go home so early did you know what was about to happen?" I already suspected that it was him but I didn't want him to know that.

"Yes. That's why I sent you home."

"H- Why."

"I didn't want you present for what I planned on doing." he obviously did it. I slightly trembled remembering the scene and the dismembered heads. This just gets better and better.

Sylas shouldn't be able to surprise me anymore but that was harder than said. Seemly even when I knew it was him it was still surprising because how can someone do that to anyone. Even as he said it now there was no remorse whatsoever in his eyes.

"You see you can't say things like that to your girlfriend." I said chuckling as I moved in my seat awkwardly. I gulped the water down my nerves sky rocketing. The water would keep me from saying something stupid. So far it's helped me in greater ways than I have ever imagined.

"I don't want to pretend to be someone I'm not. You already know who I am."

"Haile." my heart skipped a beat at the sound of my name from his lips. It scared me and aroused me. I wasn't ashamed to say that. The man was a walking God. Everything he did when he wasn't making me cry was beyond shifting.

"Yes Sylas." I now found the glass in my hand interesting but I quickly raised my eyes knowing how he didn't like that.

"Have you accepted this life?" he questioned taking a sip, his eyes never leaving mine I had to pause and remember how to breathe.

I would rather die than live like this.

The voice echoed in my head. Not so long ago I promised myself as I looked at myself in the mirror, the pain from my bum keeping me awake. I wanted to pass out. I would rather die. I cleared my throat smiling at him.

"What do mean?" I was tempted to call him Mäuschen to ease the tension but decided against it. He didn't look like he was in the mood. I had called him that once and the smirk he gave me was unsettling even though I did laugh it off. He did ask me if he looked like a Mäuschen and I had to disagree he was far from that. Way way far. I tried to argue my case of being nothing alike to the pet name he chose to give me but he won. I don't agree but he still won.

"Have you accepted your life with me?"

131

"Did you give me a choice Sylas?"

"No but have you accepted it Haile?" he asked without skipping a beat. He didn't even seem to be moved by the no that came out so strong yet calm from his mouth. No remorse whatsoever. I mastered up a smile I hoped he would buy as I nodded. I paused looking at him.

"Yes. Yes Sylas. I have accepted this life that I have no say in." I said taking a sip from my glass.

"The day I sew your mouth shut will be the last day you will ever have to worry about your mouth getting you killed." he said with the most chilling smile I've ever seen him wear. I had to lean back to try and put more distance between us, the truth behind his eyes was worrying me.

"Sylas." he didn't say anything as he watched me.

"You are scaring me."

"Baby there is nothing to be scared of if you have done nothing wrong. Come here."

he finally commanded. I made my way towards him as he looked at me. I felt his hand caress my cheek as I closed my eyes, the intensity of his stare was blinding. I finally felt his lips against mine as I held my breath. Even as I didn't feel him anymore I kept my eyes shut after composing myself when I opened them he was now by the counter, busy with something with his back turned towards me. I was finally able to breathe properly as I made my way towards my seat.

I felt like he knew something I didn't know and that worried me. The peace I felt within myself disappeared. I could feel a storm coming and I didn't know how in world I would avoid it. I eyed him for a second not getting anything from him. It was frustrating. It couldn't be Kutcher.

Sylas would have killed me weeks ago and I made sure I cleared my tracks. I needed to check up on Kutcher but more importantly I need to calm Sylas down.

...

I watched the TV screen mounted into the wall that Sylas got for me so I could watch my cooking shows and try my experiments. I looked down for a second cutting the carrots as instructed when I looked up I sucked my teeth because I didn't understand how on earth they were now busy with the flour. I didn't even look away for a second. Oh well I decided to just wing it then rewind.

This is exactly what he was talking about. Sylas didn't understand how I would make something different from the show even after watching it and making it along with them. I guess this answers that question.

Sylas cooked yesterday and I still haven't forgotten the heavy feeling he left me with. I needed to fix that. I tried to act as normal as possible as I tried to figure out what was going on with him. I spent majority of the day today at my garden. It was actually healthy and growing which brought a little happiness into my messed up world. After my garden I asked my chef if I could cook today because Sylas cooked yesterday and I wanted to do it today.

Today seemed like a busy day for him he has been in his office the whole day, we hardly had breakfast together. I couldn't help but feel antsy even though the only moment I felt like a storm was brewing within him was only yesterday. At this point I didn't actually know what to do except keep myself busy otherwise I would go insane.

"Oh that's definitely not suppose to look like that." I said looking at my work. I frowned sighing. That's what I get for winging it. I was sure Sylas would eat it anyways. I almost felt sorry for him. Almost. I slowly picked up a piece hesitant at first as I looked at it. I popped it in my mouth shutting my eyes as I slowly chewed. I opened my eyes whilst frowning, it actually wasn't that bad. Success.

I was about to make another batch when I heard footsteps. I looked up pausing I was about to smile but then I saw the look in his eyes. My legs involuntarily took a step back. The darkness in his eyes was suffocating me. I wished I could cease to exist. I could feel the fear traveling to every inch of my body. My eyes traveled from his intimidating form to the phone in his hand. My phone. I couldn't help but hold my breath, he didn't move. Deep down I knew this would be my down fall.

"I-I can explain." I whispered, tears blurred my eyes as they raced down my cheeks. He didn't even need to speak, his eyes said everything. I was too scared to question his clothing. He was in his dress shoes, pants but only a vest. He looked like he was in the middle of undressing. At this moment I regretted everything. Even though I knew damn well I didn't allow myself to slip up I covered everything, I regretted everything. The way Sylas looked at me at this moment would make anyone regret everything if they were in my shoes. I didn't know what to do.

I was too scared to run or stand from where I was standing. I could literally feel myself tremble in panic. Even though I knew deep down that if I hadn't done what I did Kutcher would be dead I couldn't help but wish I did something differently.

"Mäuschen." he called. The way that he called me was bone chilling, I would have preferred if he used my name. The pet name did nothing to hide his blood thirst. I watched him in horror as he picked up one of the clean knives from the table. His attention diverting to the knife.

"What is this?" his voice was the opposite of his eyes. Calm and levelled. At this moment I couldn't speak. I couldn't move, I couldn't breathe properly. I was slowly using my mouth to breathe. He was getting impatient and making him wait was never an option.

"Do you need help speaking?" he asked I whimpered and shook my head. He didn't seem to be with me in this moment, he was in his own world as he looked at the knife in his hand skilfully tossing it once in the air, admiring it. The tears running down my cheeks had now dampened the top of my tee, that's how much I was crying and I couldn't stop. The knife in his hand bothered me to no avail long forgotten was the phone.

I wanted to scream and plead for my life, try and make him understand my point of view, tell him my side of the story but I couldn't. I was muted by fear. I watched him move his hand swiftly and before I knew it the knife traveled at a cutting speed as it cut through the air before it went through the side of my throat.

It took me seconds to register what just happened and the immense pain that sprawled through my body bringing me to my knees as I cried and screamed in agony. I could feel the blood filling into my mouth and some of it running down my throat as my hands pressed against my throat trying to contain it. The screams of pain that left my throat seemed to die with the blood leaking from it. I was in so much of pain I couldn't move. I couldn't do anything.

All that seemed to be my least of worries as I watched Sylas still standing before me now with another knife in his hand as my eyes widened at the sight. I felt like the pain from my throat would kill me. I was in so much of pain but my heart still seemed to tighten at his sight. I wanted to beg, I wanted to scream at the paralysing pain that coursed throughout my body. At this point I would do anything to make him stop.

"I asked you a question." he stated his gaze focused on the sharp knife in his hand. I couldn't stop screaming as all I got were gurgle noises from my throat. I couldn't let out a single word. I fell down on my side as I tried moving away from him. I knew that if I didn't talk soon even though I physically couldn't he would launch the other knife to which part of my body I did not know. This was it. I didn't even fight the darkness, at least I wouldn't feel the next knife. Everything went dark as I welcomed the darkness with open arms.

...

Chapter 19

I lay in bed not moving feeling numb. Everything felt numb, I could not believe it. I of course thought I knew how ruthless Sylas could get but this left me speechless. I think I was still processing what happened and it seemed to strike a new fear into me even though I felt completely numb. I almost died. I heard the doctor tell him that whilst I was deep into slumber, my mind seemed to sense his presence every time he was close.

I think I mentally panicked every time but at the same time I felt too numb to have panic attacks, or so I thought; the speed of my racing heart seemed to triple on it's usually fast pace. I was too numb to produce anymore tears, so I just sat and stared at my walls. And by my walls I mean the white hospital room walls that were starting to make me feel like I was going crazy.

I wasn't even worried about the fact that I was going back home with him or that he took my phone so I couldn't have any contact with my mother anymore who I had been making sure to keep tabs on. I missed her, yes, we had our differences, but I truly did miss her. Sitting in this room I am not truly sure how long I have been in here, but I do know I need to stop thinking but that seems to be impossible with seeing as I woke up with an engagement band fit for a queen around my finger.

I think that was the first time in my entire life I have ever had a panic attack. Luckily, Sylas had not arrived yet, I let the nurses guide me back to my normal state of mind. Back then I could still cry, back then I could still feel the suffocating fear I had for Sylas. I avoided any mirror when the doctor finally let me go to the bathroom on my own, at first, he feared I was too dosed up on medication so I would collapse but eventually he gave me the privacy I had been craving. I did not want to see the bandage around my neck, feeling it was more than enough.

I finally concluded that I liked his mother ironic but true, right now there was no safe loved one in my life and I felt so alone. She was there, she never left the hospital. She came early and left when I fell asleep. At first, she did not say anything to me but asked me if she could sit in here with me. I had said no for the first five times. I somewhat felt it was also her fault for birthing a man worse than the devil, but she was persistent, and I was deteriorating with each day. Sylas seemed not to mind her presence. He made it clear that when he was here, she leaves us. She did not argue sensing his blood-thirst.

After some time visiting me without pushing me to speak about anything and allowing me to wallow in my numbness, she had finally spoken to me and I was surprised that I replied. She did not say anything that would have made me get her visits banned, neither did she speak about the ring on my finger. I was glad because I also didn't want to speak about it; for now, I went with if I truly believe or not truly pay attention to it, it wasn't there. That alone helped me breathe and sleep better at night.

The only thing I got from Sylas about the ring was "You have no choice." He had said as he watched me stare at it longer than necessarily, my face not showing any emotion. I of course chose to live yet again; I should have chosen death.

Sylas did not need to say much around me I understood what went through his mind, at times he lets me and on other times he does not even let me catch a glimpse of what he thinks. I have been with him for months now, I would like to convince myself that I knew part of him. He was not a very vocal person so with time I got used to it. At points like these I wish he would say something, anything. His silence was suffocating. There was nothing regretful about him which did not surprise me, if he were, he wouldn't be the man I knew. He did not apologise, instead he was still truly angry, but his anger was contained which was something new.

I guess I was now engaged. Engaged to the man I had seen myself end up with at the beginning. I would chuckle but I was afraid I would hurt myself. I was healed but I did not want to take any chances I didn't even want to touch my neck. The last time I mistakenly touched my throat I did not sleep the entire night. I felt like the medicine they had dosed up did nothing to me. I felt everything.

I was itching to ask about the ring, Sylas and I both knew that, and he wanted me to ask but I didn't have nine lives, so I decided to play it safe. Especially after his few words. It seemed as if ever since I found out about what he truly was he was always ready to hurt me, clearly, he wasn't the same man I was crazy about. Well, I wouldn't say the same because there was a side of him I had never been unlucky enough to encounter but if I wasn't inquiring about the voices in his head or his f-ed up dark side he was the same. I don't know why in the world he would think everything would go back to the way it was, I mean he is a f-ed up psychopath for crying out loud, I don't think anything would ever be normal and I don't think I will ever settle for this life.

This might sound stupid, but I would rather be stupid than be a robot. Death did not seem that bad at this point. I want to see who the fuck he thinks will marry him. I just knew deep down I would swallow my words, but I liked having the little control I had in my head, thinking Sylas is not the literally most terrifying person I have ever met. I liked convincing myself I had control over everything but that all perishes in the presence of Sylas.

At this point I couldn't even stand being in his presence, he is just so terrifying I can't even start to describe the fear that washes over me when his eyes darken whether it's in the bedroom or when he wants to make me beg for my life. I shivered changing my sleeping position. The fact that I was going back home didn't sit well with me. I quickly sat up as I watched him walk in; the room immediately turned cold.

The fact that I could sense his blood-thirst made everything more intense. I felt his eyes on me. He didn't say anything he just sat in his usual seat and stared at me. When the doctor walked in, I could finally breathe again. I dozed off as he spoke to the doctor who was also clearly intimidated, so it wasn't just me, but I had a reason as to why this man intimidated me so much and as for the doctor It was the aura that surrounded Sylas and the fact that he never smiled didn't help.

"Lets go." He simply said taking a hold of my bag that his mother had brought for me a while back. I wasn't even dressed I was still in my hospital gown and I knew he wasn't going to turn around even if I asked. I didn't want to try afraid he would make me regret even thinking about asking him that. I slowly peeled of the hospital gown; I could feel his eyes roam my body which left me with goosebumps.

...

His hand rested on my thigh as I sat quietly beside him staring at his side profile. Monsters sure are beautiful, that I had to admit, the man was beautiful in a deity way. I watched his sharp jaw move. I quickly pulled myself together realising that he was speaking.

"Would you like to go shopping with mother?" he asked his deep voice filling the car. I suddenly felt like there wasn't enough space in between us. Finally, out of the trance and realising how close he was.

"If that's okay with you." I said, he looked at me as his chest rumbled as he released a dark chuckle, I felt the need to hide from him envelope my body. I suddenly could not sit still anymore. His chuckle alone gave me flash backs.

"What are we shopping for?" I asked realising that, that should have been my first question. I was simply happy he broke his intimidating silence.

"Our engagement party." He said eyeing me. I managed to keep a straight face as I avoided his eyes which should be on the road, but I was not about to tell him that. I made peace with myself in winning the small battles between us by restraining my tongue with the promise of winning the war.

"You seem tense, are you okay Mäuschen?" he asked. Son of a-

"I'm okay just a little surprised I guess." This seemed to bring out his menacing smirk. I had to keep on reminding myself, I would not be surprised if Sylas was ten times ahead of me. Sylas knew that. It was hard containing my thoughts and I do not think I would ever be that person, but I also felt like I at least now chose my words. Because even though I would never change who I am I clearly knew that Sylas was fucked up. I had to take a deep breath in because of the conflict of contradicting myself in my head was starting to give me a headache. Even though I liked how tough I thought I was in my head whenever I looked at him all that seemed to disappear.

"About what?" he asked.

"Sylas you didn't really ask me to be your wife I just woke up with a ring I mean you ca-." I stopped myself I knew that if I continued, I would be starting something I would not be able to finish.

"Haile."

"It would have been nice if you had asked me Sylas." I concluded hoping I did not set him off. My eyes moved from him to the handle of the door. He quickly seemed to catch on as he put on the child lock.

"What's the difference, at the end there will be a wedding." At this point I wish I could say I was surprised but I was not. I could not wait to meet up with his mother. At this point in my life, I wasn't scared of dying while trying.

"Did you maybe have a different ending in mind?"

"Of course not." I said facing forward. I watched the road ahead. I somehow didn't feel like I was trapped or in jail when I was back at my kidnappers abode. I don't know why but the feeling of being imprisoned wasn't there, maybe it came every once in a while, when Sylas reminds me, I'm not allowed to go anywhere without him or a bodyguard.

"Would that make you happy?"

"Yes Sylas."

"Marry me Haile." Just wow.

For a second, I thought about the question and I gulped. It was a heavy question. I tried diverting my mind from the fact that he didn't even say please neither did he sound like he was asking but the question strongly hung in my head, I won't lie I've thought about this day, but I didn't envision it like this. His smile drew me out of my thoughts.

"Having second thoughts Mäuschen?" he was so evil.

"No Sylas I'm not." The man lacked patience.

"-Yes, Sylas I will marry you." I said knowing he wouldn't be calm and understanding for long.

"Sylas do you love me? Marriage is sacred and is entered by parties who are madly in love with each other." I said after a minute of silence, I zoned out for a second thinking about everything. The reality of my situation sinking in. I looked at his pure intense blue eyes at this moment. Every good memory of ours played at the back of my head.

"Do you love me Sylas?" I questioned as my eyes glazed over. We have been through so much together before he turned into this monster. I don't think I would have ever accepted his profession, but I was really all for him. Just his presence made me feel at home. It was that deep.

"I don't think so." He said and for some reason my heart dropped. I don't know why. I suddenly felt a slight pain on my chest that I couldn't explain neither would I question. I shifted in my seat. I wasn't supposed to be this affected; have I also gone mad?

" -Love is not enough of a word to describe what I feel for you." My stupid heart that he would most definitely tear out one day skipped. One losing their minds must be contagious because I have clearly lost it. I wasn't focused on that rushing warm emotion that flooded my entire body. It was the deep chilling fear that came with the emotion that left me frozen. It was stronger than the unneeded stupid emotion; it completely drowned it out.

I couldn't tear my eyes of him. I carefully watched every part of his upper body as his hand on the starring wheel turned the wheel as he checked the mirror, doing everything so effortlessly and in a sexy manner. His sharp jaw seemed tense. He did not look at ease as he usually did. Even his side profile was beautiful. The man was truly something else. Images of the first time he kissed me flooded my mind as I tried burying horrific thoughts of him. Sylas was bold, demanding and dominant. It was a hell of attractive, frustrating and scary. I have never met any man like him. I had quickly got addicted to his scent, being in his arms and him.

"You do know that you will end up killing me one day right." I said sniffing. I could not help but sniff at the memories. I felt like he was going to break me, emotionally, mentally and physically. And he might have succeeded. I did not want to think about the knife that he threw into my neck. It was more than enough that it gave me sleepless nights in the hospital, his presence alone gave me sleepless nights.

"I won't kill you. I won't ever kill you."

"What made you change your mind?"

"You."

I was surprised yet still skeptical. I did not believe this. Sylas was pure evil.

"You almost killed me."

"I know."

"-continue with your ways, I will bring you to the brink of death and make you beg me to kill you." He said chuckling to himself before eyeing me yet again and that was the last thing that was said in the car. I was done. It was now clear to me that I would rather die trying than to let myself get to that point.

I urgently needed to speak with his mom.

Past.

I looked at the long stairway taking in a deep breath. I could feeling the shaking of my fingers. It wasn't the long stairway that made me so nervous and ignited so much fear inside me. It was what was down the stairway. I had to keep the smile on my face, not only for the man waiting for me down the stairway but also for our esteemed guests now all watching me.

I slowly walked down the steps taking my time and keeping my eyes on him and him alone. I was so nervous. All of my friends and family- which only consisted of my mother- were here. Sylas has been in a crazy good mood today, I think I might have seen him smile at someone who wasn't me once today but maybe I was seeing things. I was uneasy.

I didn't like this change of mood from him, he was a very fucked up person and him suddenly changing like this was bad for everyone in this room, myself included. I didn't want to do anything to provoke him, I wasn't willing to take any chances. I don't think I could take anymore psychotic behaviour from Sylas. I was tired, both physically and mentally.

Above all I was relieved Kutcher wasn't here. I didn't want to lose anyone close to me to this psychopath. I had to make sure nothing went wrong there was too much at stake.

He has been awfully quiet the past few days. I was hesitant on going with his mother to search for a dress for my engagement party. I thought maybe I would catch a small sign of nervousness from him seeing as I would be spending so much of time alone with his mother. We could plan everything perfectly behind his back. But there was nothing not even a single shred of nervousness in him. Instead I was the nervous one between us.

While shopping with his mother she didn't once bring it up. She had promised me she would not bring up or speak about anything that would make me uncomfortable and I was grateful for that. Aside from everything his mother was just like her son. I could see so much of resemblance between them in character. Except she wasn't as batshit crazy like her son. I still kept some kind of distance because at this point I trusted no one at that kind of level but my views on her seemed to change for the better.

I didn't quite understand her but aside from Anita, who after doing a double check on me and decided I was no threat, had no problem with me anymore. Her mother was just crazy as her father if not more. Apparently Sylas' father killed her then boyfriend and she ended up killing his supposed fiancé that he wasn't even going to marry because of her. I, myself, don't even know how that turned into love. That was part of the reason why I stayed wary of her too. Cause just because I haven't seen her crazy side doesn't mean she doesn't have one.

I didn't even wish to have a two minute talk with her husband his aura was just like his sons only Sylas was not really a peoples person. His father seemed to know how to socialise but he also never smiled. Ha, it must be a family thing. His brother seemed normal out of the family, he was clearly the most outgoing but he gave me chills because I felt like he was the type to kill people while smiling. Smiling was something he wasn't afraid to do but there was just something about his smile.

The family I was about to marry into willingly was clearly something out of a nightmare. I must have been a serial killer in my previous life. I tried convincing Sylas marriage was a sham but he seriously believes in it and I felt things would definitely change after we got married. He took marriage seriously. I didn't understand why because he didn't know the first thing about sanity and love.

The white lavish silky dress I had on now seemed heavier than before. It was really beautiful but I wasn't fully on board with it because I felt like it gave me a preview on what was about to happen. Sylas' mother has already started addressing the wedding facade. I honestly wasn't there. My steps seemed to falter and my heart beat picked up. I was close to getting to Sylas. Too close. I watched his blue eyes trained on me, a shiver running down my spine. The way he was looking at me I was a hundred percent sure that not even in my wildest dreams would he let me go.

I could feel the many eyes on me as I took my slow and conscious steps downstairs my eyes solely on the man waiting for me. I was scared my anxiety would make me trip and fall so I had to be careful and slow. The gaze from the audience didn't hold a candle to Sylas' strong gaze. I took his hand into mine as he met me on the last step. Immediately his hand wrapped around my waist as he possessively pulled me closer to him. I complied, his scent sending bells in my head.

My mother seemed very happy and pleased about Sylas. Surprised at first but very much pleased. At this point I didn't care as long as she was happy and as long as she thought I was in good hands I was more than content. I didn't want her involved. I would rather die than to get her involved. Yes we had our disagreements but for the life of me I couldn't even bare the thought of anything bad happening to her.

She seemed so happy, she was socialising with Sylas' family. At this point I felt like a little girl again I wanted to cry in her arms and tell her all my problems so she could easily wipe my tears and problems away. Weirdly I wished my dad was here. I wish he could also see me at my engagement party even though he wouldn't be happy of the circumstances neither was I but I just wanted him to see the woman he raised. I missed him so much.

I took in a deep breath closing my eyes for a second telling myself my friends and family just need to make it out of that big door. I needed to compose myself. I needed to be on my A game. I innocently smiled as I looked up as Sylas feeling his gaze on me. His eyes were terrifying. The hue of his eyes seemed to intensify the darkness in them.

I ignored my racing heart and faced the audience. Everyone was coming to us with congratulations, of course with no idea what happens behind the curtains. I was sure that even if they did know they wouldn't be able to help, they would be forced to turn the other way. It was pretty clear how powerful the Harmans were, even if one didn't know about their empire in the dark world. They had the kind of power that was well known without a doubt.

...

I was proud of myself. Actually more than proud, I was able to make everyone happy all at once including my psychopath of a fiancé, which never seemed to possible these days. Even though I never really understood why Onetta would have insinuated that I have a child, I never really held anything against her, although I had decided to stay clear of everyone. Watching from afar she wasn't one to dabble in anyone's business but her family's safety was her priority.

When I say she minds her own business I mean Sylas could literally drag me across the kitchen with my hair while Onetta sat on one of the chairs eating her food and going through her phone. I was obviously mad at first but then I realised I shouldn't expect any sort of help or anything from people I don't know. At times I liked that she minded her own business.

I lifted the slender glass filled with spiked juice to my lips, oh how I had missed my alcohol. As I was sitting down on one of the tables with the cold wind brushing against my exposed skin, the party continued outside, I froze adjusting my eyes. It couldn't be. Maybe I was seeing things. I choked quickly holding my breath and tried to control my coughing.

I had asked Sylas to take a minute to myself I was tired of standing and socialising. I was glad he understood and let me sit because I felt like I would faint. I looked around trying to see if anyone else saw me choking. When I caught no one staring, my eyes moved back to the man in a black suit in the house. I could see him through the glass sliding door. There were people around him and he was far but I knew exactly who he was. Kutcher.

I looked at Sylas, and then looked back at the man looking at me. My legs couldn't move. If I decided not to move and go to him then Sylas would not be able to make up a reason to put me back in hospital. But I had to warn him. I had to warn him about everything and tell him face to face that he had to let everything go including myself. I watched him subtly motion for me to follow. I quivered in fear my eyes slowly trailing to Sylas. I couldn't.

I couldn't move. My mind went to Sylas actually seeing him here. I knew I would somehow be blamed and harmed, I had to get him out of here as soon as possible. But what if Sylas caught me while I was with him and got the wrong idea. My head was buzzing. Maybe Kutcher would stay in the shadows and leave if I ignored him. My head buzzed a little. I had secretly drunk tonight, there was too much pressure I wouldn't have been able to get through it sober.

I wish. I knew Kutcher and I knew he would never do that. There was a greater chance of him coming to me and exposing himself if I ignored him. I could feel my leg start to shake in frustration. There was no peaceful outcome in any scenario involving Sylas and Kutcher in my mind. I was screwed. I had to act now and I had to act fast.

Without thinking I slowly got up and discreetly moved towards him. I followed him without question; the way not even clear anymore because I just needed to speak to him. I can't believe I had to think about warning him. He has always been there for me and I was a hundred percent sure that if he was in my shoes he would do the same. I felt tears rush down my face as I thought about us. We have been through so much I still wanted to see him settle down and have kids and everything. I couldn't believe my life.

I walked into the room with no sense of direction as I wiped the tears. I jumped turning around when the bang of the door sounded across the room. I watched him look at me. Emotions rushing through his eyes. I couldn't keep away anymore as I jumped into his arms. I thought he would push me away but he embraced me with so much warmth I started sobbing in his arms. They felt warm and safe.

When I took a whiff of his cologne my body immediately relaxed. His arms felt so familiar and warm I couldn't help but tighten my arms around him. A minute passed, the silence between us comforting as I lay my head on his chest. I wanted to savour this moment. I wanted it to last forever. I don't remember the last time I felt this safe or at peace.

"We need to go." his voice filled the room making me gulp still hooked to him. I slowly released myself from his embrace.

"Kutcher. It was nice seeing you and we don't have time but you need to leave and forget about me. You need to leave and never look back." I said my eyes solely focused on his.

"I'm not leaving this place without you. I can't for the life of me understand why you are here, I have my suspicions but we will talk once we get out of here. Haile what you need to understand is that I will not leave without you." I felt like I was getting stabbed in the chest countless of times. I could feel my chest tightening up.

"Kutch-"

"Why are you here?" he asked slowly. Didn't he just- he wouldn't understand, he would never understand he would rather die fighting. Sylas would kill him.

I didn't want to lie, I didn't want to put his life at risk but I also knew the truth would do him no good. He's a Detective he knows how powerful Sylas is he was just stubborn but so was Sylas and Sylas killed people. Sylas is a monster that I wanted nowhere close to anyone I cared about.

I stood for a minute contemplating what to do. Should I tell him the truth or lie. I didn't like lying to him it felt suffocating but I also didn't want to lose him. Would he believe me if I said I'm in love. Would he believe me if I said I was here on my own accord. I highly doubted it and I didn't want him to view me as a different person but his life was more important to me than what he thought of me.

For a second being mean to him and shutting him out occurred to me but I knew that wouldn't work. It didn't work before why would it work now. I remember needing peace and just wanting to be alone. I was hurting, it was after a huge fight with my mom and I decided to go to my dad's cabin. I felt like I couldn't do whatever I was doing with her anymore.

Kutcher followed me all the way there. He didn't seem to understand that I wanted to be alone even though at the time It wasn't good for my mental health, alcohol was my only companion. I just wanted to drown my sorrows and forget. Kutcher seemed persistent and annoying at the time. I tried being mean and distant but he didn't leave in fact I think that encouraged him even more to get to me.

So much was running through my head but I concluded that lying to him seemed the best option right now but I still didn't think he would believe me. I blinked a few times looking into his eyes, I needed to get this right. I needed to do this for him. It doesn't matter how much I despised doing it. It was for him and at this point I would do anything to get him out of here alive.

"I-" it was harder than I thought. I was disappointed in myself. I realised I was just taking myself in circles we didn't have time. I thought at this point I would have mastered the art of deceit but clearly not. The words were stuck in my throat. I felt so much pressure, my head was pounding. I had to hurry up and get him out of here plus my inner self was having a battle with myself. The thought of lying to him seemed harder than I anticipated.

"I don't have an explanation but you have to trust me." My tongue seemed to have a mind of it's own. He didn't seem touched by my words. I took a deep breath and took a step towards him taking his hands into mine. That seemed to grab his attention.

"Kutcher. I can't tell you why I am here but I need you to leave. I have my reasons as to why I'm here and I need you to trust me. I need you to leave and never look back." I said making sure to look him in the eye, he needed to understand how serious I was.

"No. We both know how dangerous it is to be here. Let's go and you know I will not be leaving without you." my head seemed to be spinning. What part of- I didn't understand why he wouldn't listen and leave. Couldn't he see the desperation and fear in my eyes. I moved from him pouring myself a drink and pushing it back. I closed my eyes for a second enjoying the slight burn at the back of my neck. The noise in my head seemed to quieten down a bit.

"Months Haile. Months. I have so many questions but I would prefer asking you them once we are out of this house." his voice seemed heavy and sad. I understood why he would feel this way but I was more aggravated that he wouldn't see how desperately I needed him to comply with me right now.

The alcohol in my system seemed to give me the push I needed. I was ready to bend over lying, I didn't feel so heavy inside anymore thinking about it. I just needed to make him believe that I would leave with him, that was easier than pushing him away. I was tempted to pour another one but I stopped I didn't need Sylas finding out I had alcohol. Sylas!

I tried controlling the panic that flooded my body at the thought of his name. When I looked up I realised Kutcher had been speaking and he was now closer than I would prefer. I felt like Sylas was always watching me. I moved back. We have spent more than enough borrowed time in here. I was sure Sylas would start looking for me any second now we had to leave. Maybe I could slip him out. Everyone was outside. I looked at Kutcher, I didn't have time for this.

"Okay Let's go." I said looking at him straight in the eye. A bad feeling from the pits of my stomach spread throughout my body like wild fire I had to take a deep breath in to compose myself. The care and love in his eyes was also overwhelming. I felt like shit. But I would rather I feel like shit than to see him slaughtered in front of me.

"I'm sorry. Kutcher. I'm sorry for everything. I promise to explain everything when we get home. Let's go." he didn't seem relieved as I thought he would be.

"Haile. Whatever is going on I promise to help you. You know I would never let you down. Talk to me." he said. I'm sure he could see the tears brimming in my eyes. Not now. I had to compose myself. I thought everything was going according to plan. I didn't want him throwing questions at me right now. I don't understand why he decided to ask now because he said he would wait until we were out of here. Which wasn't going to happen.

"I know. I trust you. Somethings are just hard getting out. I missed you." I genuinely said looking at him. I saw him let down his guard vulnerability filling his eyes.

"I missed you too." he said pulling me into an emotional hug. I didn't want to let go. I felt like this would be the last time I will ever hug him. I felt like sobbing but I held my sobs back letting a few tears flow down my cheeks.

"After we leave we will go to my brothers Island where we will be untraceable because I know you wouldn't be in this house willingly. If it's money they want I will gladly give it to them but we will never set foot on their land ever again." he said his hands on my cheeks as he looked at me while speaking. Every word he spoke felt so promising. I couldn't help the little faith and hope I felt at the moment. I knew better but I couldn't help but dream.

I slowly nodded my head as he smiled at

me before kissing my forehead. I lead him out making sure to release his hand once we were out of the room. I looked around for any sign of trouble as we went down the hallway. I had a bad feeling in my stomach. I could still hear the soft music coming from outside.

When we reached the top of the stairway I realised there wasn't a soul downstairs where a few people had lingered earlier on. I stood still feeling my soul leave my body, I had spoken too soon. Sylas stood alone with this big sharp sword in his hand. The way he held it made it look like it belonged in his hand. He wasn't smirking nor smiling. At this instant I wished I wasn't living. I couldn't even turn around to look at Kutcher. I was so petrified I forgot how to breathe.

After that everything seemed to be a blur I somehow blacked out when I came back the sight of Sylas slicing Kutcher open paralysed me. I seemed to be going in and out of consciousness. Everything was buzzing. I couldn't move. I was somehow on the floor. I assumed it was sobs that came out of mouth as my hearing seemed to be broken I couldn't hear a sound but I was sure of the sound that I was producing as I watched Sylas wrap Kutcher's intestines around my neck as he dragged me somewhere. I couldn't do anything. I was paralysed in fear. I couldn't even speak. The way Sylas was looking at me convinced me he would kill me.

He wasn't making a sound, my hearing

was back and there was dead silence around us. The only sound I could hear was coming from my mouth. My eye sight was dark. The image of him slicing Kutcher open replaying in my head. I could feel his blood all over me. And just like that everything became dark. When my sight came back. His mom was taking me somewhere. When we walked into the room Kellita was there and she immediately embraced me and held me as I cried. I didn't know what was going on. I felt so alone, scared and confused.

I felt like I was dreaming I couldn't believe what I just saw. My heart rate spiked up as everything kept on replaying itself in my mind. I seemed to have passed out because when I woke up again it was just me and Sylas. I couldn't speak. I think I forgot how to speak I couldn't remember what to do if I wanted to beg for my life. I couldn't move. All I could do was cry. I couldn't recognise where I was and that scared me even more. There was a dead look in Sylas' eyes. The only thing heavily running through my mind was how much I wished I was dead.

Present

I quivered trying to focus on the blood in my mouth that developed from bitting my lip too hard, trying to stop the sounds coming from my mouth. I could feel him deep inside me. I felt like I could feel him in my chest. My eyes were sore from crying. My whole body was sore. I now knew that there was something as too much pleasure. Too much pleasure leads to pain if repeated over and over and over again.

My fingers dug into his chest. I wanted to stop breathing. I had to keep the pace otherwise there would be consequences. I didn't want a repeat of the two last times. I was hurt. I was so hurt and tired. Orgasm after orgasm. I get it, he was punishing me. I left him, but I had to. He doesn't seem to understand that he is a psychotic murderer whom I don't want to be in the same space of air with.

Sylas didn't even want me to go to the bathroom for more than five minutes. It's been sex after sex. On top of sex. Even when we had a break to eat when he remembered that I was a human being that had needs. He would still look at me like he wanted to devour me alive as if he hadn't just spent the last few hours before in between my legs.

I regretted leaving. Yes at this moment I wish I could take it back, I knew this was just the beginning. Just the thought of what happened the last time scared me. I couldn't sleep for weeks after what he did to me. After everything that happened with Kutcher I think I lost a piece of myself and Sylas really gave me another proper definition of monster after that. A new definition of pain.

It was three days, the most dreadful three days of my life, to me it felt like weeks but his mother said I had been with him for three days. That was when I was properly introduced back to into panic attacks and when I finally got my first dose of real nightmares.

It was just me and him in that room. I could feel the tightening of my stomach I wanted to slow down but the grip of his hands on my thighs where I already had his handprints, tightened. His blue eyes daring me. I couldn't stop crying. The darkness in his eyes didn't once fade ever since I got here. I shook, my entire being being shifted as I fought for my breath after reaching my orgasm.

At this point I wanted to get out of here even knowing that what comes next after this would surely leave me only partially sane. I paused feeling my body give up on me.

"Sylas- I can't- ple-" I didn't get to finish as one of my wounds were reopened. I screamed. I felt like I would choke on my sobs as my neck tightened up. I clashed my teeth together swallowing the wails that gnawed at my throat.

If I didn't have a drinking problem maybe I wouldn't be here. Maybe Kutcher would still be alive, maybe the memory of him being gutted alive in front of me wouldn't replay in my head minute after minute. After he had taken me from Kellita he wasn't pleased either about my drinking. I remember swearing on my life that I would never touch it ever again, I kept that promise when I still strongly valued my life.

"Would you like to continue with that sentence Mäuschen?" he asked. I didn't want this, it was unbearable. I lost in his sick game, nothing new there but I had at least hoped and prayed it would be better than being caged in the shower with nowhere to go, just being slammed against the glass as he took me from behind. At the beginning I had almost preferred this from what Sylas had been doing to me. I was chasing every breath. With every movement I was slowly losing.

I wanted to be done. I wanted to go back with him if that's what it took to make him stop. I hated this bed. I knew deep down that after Sylas was done with me, back home I would either not be the same ever again, or I wouldn't be breathing. I didn't mind losing my mind maybe I would be able to sleep at night again but I definitely didn't want to find out what he would do to me this time.

I couldn't do it anymore but I knew he could easily make things worse if I quit now. My body wanted a break, it needed a break. I was beyond exhausted but Sylas looked like he was just getting started.

"Sylas- may- I please- use the bathroom." I panted.

"Hold it." he said flipping us over.

"Sy-Sylas I-I- please I- Please. I- ahhh." at a certain point I didn't even remember what I was begging for when he entered me, but I just knew I couldn't stop. And so I didn't and at that point I felt like speaking or opening my mouth somehow made the pain bearable.

That's all we have been doing for the past week. Not that I saw the light and darkness outside to confirm that the day was over, I would see the day and time on his phone passing by. I was scared to even blink, breathe or speak in his presence. He was pissed yet so calm about everything. Sometimes he would skill into his head while we were having sex I would scream for him but to no avail because his eyes looked beyond empty. I was terrified of those moments.

The last time I screamed so much I thought my voice box would never be the same again. The next morning my voice came out shaky. We were still at the asylum and I had made the discovery that this place would be decorated with dead bodies.

The entire week there was no use of protection and I wouldn't ask him about it because I never knew if that would somehow offend him or disrespect him. I would love telling him I didn't want anything to do with him but I decided I wanted a not so brutal death. I could clearly see that he was on the edge these days. Sylas was always calm and collected which is why I was terrified, his eyes seemed unhinged.

That what was my whole week consisted of. Sylas made me come, bleed, scream, shake, beg and we hadn't even reached home yet. I barely got any sleep and when I did get that little sleep I made sure to try and enjoy it. I completely wiped myself from the world and my current circumstances. I was just alone and I enjoyed that. At this point I just wanted to be alone.

I didn't mind the darkness I was somehow familiar to it. I would take any darkness in exchange to the one that floods Sylas' eyes when he looked at me letting me know to run if I thought I had the chance. I never did. And I never will unless if he told me to and there was a slim chance there too. I liked having legs. I didn't want to lose anymore of me to him.

He had asked me if I wanted to leave I didn't reply terrified to be breathe. He then opened the door for me and told me I could leave. My brain had completely shut down any glimmer of hope, as I just sat down and started crying. I didn't know how to act because I never knew with Sylas. A lot went through my brain. I was scared of even moving so I froze and cried until he decided what he wanted to do next, I had no power in this room. I never had any power when it came to Sylas.

I had tried and had successfully managed to burry some of my darkest memories with him in those three days but they seemed to be resurfacing. Every time I felt like he was definitely going to kill I am brought back to those days by my mind I couldn't control it. My life was hanging on a thread.

When his mother saw me. I knew her mind was made up. The week before my wedding I realised I didn't care that much about my life anymore. I would run whenever I got the chance. The sleepless nights or the nights I woke up because of my nightmares made me make the decision to go to his mother. She was more than happy to help me. I was scared and I didn't know where I got the courage but when I finally got away at first I felt like I was free but then things changed for the worst realising who Sylas was and that there was no turning back. I had to accept my fate. I had made my decision and I had to stand by it.

My mind seemed to stop working as shock waves shot through my body making me shake. The powerful orgasm shot through my entire body as I tightly grabbed onto the sheets my mind becoming blank and my eyes rolling to the back of my head.

...

It's nothing you can't handle. It's nothing you can't handle. I chanted to myself quietly with my eyes shut as I sat opposite him. Even with my eyes closed I could still feel his eyes on me. They burned me. His presence bringing my very soul to it's quivering knees.

A tear ran down my cheek. I now wished he hadn't left the room. After ordering me to get ready for our flight of course after him slowly. I realised I was getting closer and closer to my doom.

After he decided I could find my rest then, I couldn't move. I literally couldn't move my limbs. They were shaking and unresponsive to me. Sylas had disappeared into the bathroom for five minutes I had foolishly closed my eyes and hoped he would never come back. He came back. He had scooped me up and placed me in a sweet scented tub full of warm water and bubbles. I was surprised he remembered just how I liked my water close to hot but not too hot. That was warm for me.

I still didn't think that the other rooms in this asylum were the same as this one. This was like an apartment, a five star apartment. And there was so much of Sylas in here that I doubted that this was his first or second time here. But why would he have a room inside an asylum. There was a lot I couldn't seem to put together because I know and can bet my life on the fact that Sylas would never come here for himself seeking help neither would anyone check him in here without his consent. None of this made sense.

I expected him to drop me in and leave, scratch that I had hoped for it but he got in on the other side. He had took his own sweet time as he bathed me and kissed me here and there, being gentle throughout. Even though he was gentle I couldn't help but jump every now and then, he didn't seem to mind. That didn't seem to even make him feel a little bad or guilty.

It was like he was analysing my body seeing if it was still how he had left it. To see if I had bruised or changed what belonged to him. To see if anyone had touched what belonged to him. I held my breath. There was nothing he would find but I was still scared. I didn't trust anything at this point not even myself. In other news I was truly grateful the hickey was gone, my neck was still healing. Sylas had scraped it off. I cried just thinking about it. I quickly wiped my tears looking away.

I remember holding my breath and closing my eyes for the longest time even as I had felt him get behind me and gently laid my upper body onto his hard chest. I had finally found my breath after some time. We had sat like that for a while as he also made sure the water stayed the same temperature. After that I was confident again that I could maybe sleep without nightmares. I had felt a little relaxed, my body, my body had felt a little relaxed. I find it necessary to correct myself.

After getting dressed and waiting for him with a blank mind that had then wanted no sleep, even though I was a little at peace knowing he was outside that door maybe even outside the asylum, having no idea when he would return. When he came back I wouldn't have guessed, even when he made the first call telling whom I had guessed was Kairo that he was done and was coming home. The second call, I didn't know neither did I have guesses whom it was. I just know he told them to bring the clean up crew. I had too much of my shit to deal with than to hang onto those words.

As we stepped outside his door I then realised the amount of dead bodies covering the floor. So many dead people. I had been confused as to why I hadn't heard any commotion, I had then realised what the phone calls where about. I tried keeping a strong face and walking but I failed miserably, it wasn't everyday that I saw so many dead bodies, or any at that.

"Mäuschen don't look so shocked this is all your doing. The five targets I initially had didn't seem to satisfy my hunger," he paused as he held my cheek I couldn't look at him. Even after every thing he was too close. He then made me look at him.

"And I couldn't return to you with that hunger. I don't want to kill you and I don't want break anything, yet. I would rather we sort our issues out at home." he said his hand easily sliding around my waist as he pulled me closer to him. He gently pecked my lips before leading the way.

I have always been such a nice person. Was this because for that period of time when I hated mothers guts, but I've never actually disrespected her. Even in our arguments I avoided raising my tone or being disrespectful so why. Was it because of the alcohol but I needed it to keep me sane because of my mother

I didn't deserve this, I wasn't having a pity party for myself but I didn't deserve this. I remember barely making my legs work as his hand had tightened around my waist, after seeing one too many dead bodies I seemed to have lost my sight. I couldn't see properly my eye sight was filled with white. I took a deep breath in pulling myself out of the horrific memories as I tried to relax.

I couldn't seem to get the hang of relaxing, his stare was making things worse. I was afraid of going to sleep because I fear he would join me in the bedroom and I couldn't take anymore. I leaned against the seat staring into nothing. I couldn't relax even if I tried because I knew that sooner or later this jet would land and I knew I wouldn't like what Sylas had in store for me.

...

The moment the plane landed, I thought I would have a panic attack. Everything seemed to go on at a very fast pace as he took my hand and lead me to the awaiting cars. Even as he pulled me closer to him in the car I let him. I was so scared. I felt like saying I was scared was an understatement. Sylas seemed like a brand new person as we reached his homeland.

The craziness that was so exposed to me before was now behind those blue eyes of his eyes. One would think I wouldn't have anymore tears to cry. As the gates to our home came into view my hand wrapped around his. I looked at him, my lips trembling. He looked at our intertwined hands raising a brow.

"Do you love me Sylas?" my hoarse voice whispered out. Tears now wetting my lips. He kept quiet looking at me. I felt like he was looking at my soul. I looked down at my trembling hands.

"Please forgive me Sylas." the car had now stopped, it was time to get out. I watched him signal for the driver to stop as he was about to open the door.

"I'm so so sorry. I'm sorry. I'm sorry." I couldn't seem to say any other sentence aside from this one.

"Why are you sorry Haile." it didn't sound like a question but it was a question. I felt my chest tighten up as his eyes darkened.

"I only left because I was scared Sylas -I ran from you. I-I- didn't choose-"

"You chose to listen to my mother." he said chuckling, the atmosphere was getting thicker by the second.

" No no I didn't. I thought you would end up killing me. The last time-"

"Have I ever went back on my word." he asked.

"N-no." I said thinking back and finally answering him.

"But I-"

"Let's go." he said ending the conversation if I could even call it that. He opened the door getting out before he held out his hand for me to take. I softly placed trembling hand on his. I followed him as he lead me into the house. The memories flooded into my head as I walked in. As I was away I almost missed almost burning down his kitchen and making him eat my horrible experiments.

I smiled wiping away my unending tears. He lead us to his office. I followed without question. When we entered the office there was a man whom I'd never seen before already sitting in one of the stools and his brother Kairo was sitting on the couch with a drink in his hand more than comfortable. He smiled at our presence. Upon seeing Sylas they stood in respect before sitting again.

Everything stopped as they spoke about something, this loud ringing took over in my ears as I stood. What was going on.

"Mäuschen." His voice brought me back. I looked at all of them looking at me as I was the only one standing, I watched Kairo look at my arms and neck before chuckling and muttering something in German to his brother. Sylas' handprints and marks were all over me.

I looked at Sylas with tears in my eyes. I looked at the stool next to the man and the couch, there was still space left next to Kairo. I took a deep breath in and walked over to the other side of the table and stood next to Sylas. I could tell I definitely made the right decision as I sat on his lap not looking at anyone in the room.

I could hear them speaking but I couldn't hear a word. Ever since we landed here I wasn't really sure what was going on in my head. I was pulled back into the world when papers were placed in front of me. Confused I looked up at Sylas. He didn't say anything but just handed me a pen. I was scared to ask but I had to. Before I could say anything Kairo spoke up lifting up his glass to me with a smile on his face.

"Welcome to the family." he had said making me look at Sylas.

"Sylas." I whispered looking back at the papers in front of me, realising what they were. I started panicking.

"This isn't up for debate. You can either sign now or I will tell them to get out and call them back when you think I have convinced you enough to sign." My heart raced as my grip on the pen tightened. I looked at my bandaged fingers shivering.

"Sylas- I- "

"In case you don't make it, I want you to die as Mrs Harman." he said.

"You said you wouldn't kill me."

"You said you would never leave me." he said. Even though I knew he would never go back on his word I was still shaken to the core. I looked at the marriage license in front of me. The man sitting opposite us showed me where I had to sign Sylas had already signed. My hand trembled as I tried to contain myself.

I knew sooner or later Sylas would get impatient and kick everyone out and wouldn't listen to me after that no matter how much I would promise to sign them, asking for another chance. At that thought I signed my soul away as a tear dropped onto the paper making a tiny stain on my signature. I felt a hole in my stomach. It's not like I had a choice but what did I just do.

I took a deep breath in reminding myself it's useless to fear the inevitable. It's been about four hours that I got home and Sylas hasn't touched a single hair on my head. I should be grateful I was still alive, I am, at least I think I am. The anticipation was killing me and the new ring on my finger wasn't helping my situation.

Even though I wanted to dislike the ring I couldn't help but find it pretty, under different circumstances I would have loved it. He seemed to love it on my finger. A few hours ago in the kitchen I noticed that if he was looking at me he was looking at the ring. After the whole soul robbing ordeal he asked me to make him one of my experiments. Sylas was fucking crazy.

I knew either way there was no way I would be pardoned for what I did and I didn't understand what he was doing. I just knew that fear and anxiousness were not a good combination. I didn't know or understand anything going on in my life anymore except that if I died anytime soon it would be by my husbands hand. How lucky of me.

I didn't understand why he wanted me to make him something because as some people get better at things I was literally getting worse. I wish he could cook me something I missed his cooking but I wasn't about to let him know that. He had sat not far from me as I started working hoping that there would be no fire this time. Maybe I will get lucky and he would be hospitalised for food poisoning, I didn't want his death on my conscious.

Of course there almost was an explosion and of course there was fire and I almost burnt myself, it's been a while since I've done anything in the kitchen obviously aside from the fact that I was terrible. Sylas managed to help me not get burnt of course he wanted me unharmed for when he would start his own torture. I served him his plate, I was skeptical about serving myself it looked promising but I knew myself.

He had this power to make everything going on seem okay for that moment. I let myself have these forgetful moments because honestly it was now my escape. I can't escape the inevitable. So if pretending for a second will let me be able to breathe normally once again I would take that chance.

Sylas didn't miss a heartbeat in eating it. I couldn't understand the trust he had in me even I didn't trust myself. Plus I think he enjoyed watching me burn down his kitchen. When he knew it was safe to eat he made me eat with him. Just like old times. I know that he could tell that his presence brought fear to my very soul but he didn't care. Oh and it wasn't as bad as I thought it would be, I felt like everything I did now mattered. So I was kind of happy that after all that I actually kind of enjoyed one of my experiments. That only happened once in a blue moon.

I looked at myself in the full length mirror, the dark green dress I had on made my skin glow. For a minute I wasn't staring at the dress anymore I was staring at the marks Sylas left at least they weren't as visible as three days ago but they were still visible seeing as Kairo spotted them. Before Kairo left he informed Sylas about his parents ordering everyone's presence. I thought I was definitely not going but here I was all dressed and ready to go.

I sighed pushing my hair behind my ear. I slightly lifted up my dress it was beautiful and long enough to cover my feet but not long enough to touch the ground. A fancy dress for a fancy dinner. I looked at my pretty toes in the black heels at least I really loved my shoes they had cute little diamond designs on them. I think these were my favourite shoes.

I stopped thinking about the whole thing and just told myself to accept that Sylas was the one in control so now I just went with the flow it was either that or I would go crazy. Every time he came close I had to bite my tongue because apologising is all I wanted to do. I know it wouldn't change anything but I couldn't help but ask for forgiveness. I don't think anyone could understand how much I feared this man and what he was capable of.

I slightly jumped when I felt hands on my waist looking up at the mirror, Sylas' reflection smiled at me. It was a beautiful smile. He pulled me back closer to his body as my head rested on his chest, I took in a shaky breath seeing my body start to slightly tremble at how close he was.

"You are breathtaking Mrs Harman." he said kissing my neck making me jump.

"Thank you." I didn't understand what was going on and I wouldn't ask. He lightly kissed my neck before looking up at me in the mirror, getting serious.

"Have I ever made you happy?" he asked. I took a deep breath in calming my racing heart. I didn't understand the question I didn't think he cared and I didn't think he would ever give a single flying fuck to even considering my emotions. I knew the second one was true because I was going to ask Sylas to let me go and consider my feelings anyone in the side lines looking at us would laugh.

I was about to answer honestly with a no. If I die I die. But all these memories came flooding back. I had no doubt in my mind that Sylas would do anything for me beside let me go as we speak he built me yes from scratch my own ice rink. When he showed me I was happy, surprised and scared, just how powerful was this person.

The cooking shows that I held for him in the kitchen, which were full of shit honestly because I would sometimes pretend I was on a cooking show and telling my audience- Sylas, who would make sure to make time for them even when coming from work- my ingredients which I would sometimes say out loud in a questionable manner. I chuckled thinking of all the fires I've started in the kitchen.

Sylas told me I should just get out every time it happened, he would handle it. He didn't want me anywhere near fire he almost made me stop my experiments but I was grateful he didn't he made sure I had supervision though. He has never once said any of my experiments tasted like shit even though I wouldn't eat most of them because I valued my life. Yes the bad outweighed the good but when we were good we were so good.

I remember teaching him how to skate. It was a very comical few days. I enjoyed knowing and being good at something he wasn't, even though he wasn't as bad as I was at first. I did force him to learn he preferred watching me on the side lines but I insisted. He only did it for three days and continued to watch me do my thing, he would come in every once in a while after some blackmailing from my side.

Sylas had not so many different sides to him. And of course with the flowers he never stopped and I don't think he ever will. I loved them the most, they reminded me that the type of person that Sylas was when he wasn't losing his mind was still there. I wasn't trying to hold on to false hope because I let that ship sink a long time ago, it just helped me sleep better at night. My garden had grown over time, it was beautiful.

"Can I be honest?" I asked looking at him through the mirror as his eyes solemnly focused on me.

"Go on." he said curiosity flooding his eyes.

"You do make me happy but- there is no true happiness without the feeling of safety- only moments." I said looking at him trying to see if I needed to start running or begging. I didn't like any memory anymore because a good one is always accompanied by a bad one and so was it the other way around.

"Safety?"

"Sylas I feel safe with you but I'm not safe from you." I said softly. I felt like a weight was lifted from my shoulders for some reason. After a long pause of us staring at each other through the mirror he kissed my cheek and took my hand saying nothing as he led me to the car I was guessing. We were on our way to his mother's mandatory dinner.

I had a lot of questions floating through my mind, did she know I was back, did she know what Sylas has been up to and would she try something with Sylas. I didn't know if I wanted her to or not, I was already dead anyways why should I settle. Why should I have to live like this, because you wouldn't want to keep on getting caught and Sylas making it worse every single time. I didn't want to live like that.

...

I sat quietly beside him as we sat at the back of the limo. He hasn't struck yet but I knew I wasn't off the hook this just meant it will be the worst thing I've ever experienced. I let out a wavering breath. I closed my eyes before opening them at least I would see his mother one last time, the person who actually tried to help me.

"Sylas why haven't you done anything to me yet?" I asked bravely looking at him.

"Is there a slim chance that you have maybe possibly found it in your h-heart to forgive me?-" I had to try. I found it harder to let out the word heart than the question alone. I couldn't stop thinking about this even if I already knew the answer I had to ask.

"No." he said before chuckling.

"You have always been impatient Mäuschen, this time around I think you should think otherwise." that was the only thing he said and I strangely found myself content and accepting. More than before. It was better from the horses mouth.

The car arrived at his parents grand mansion that I never seemed to get used to no matter how many times I was to come back. I let him take my hand as he led us inside. Everyone and everything was just simply existing around me I just wanted to see his mother. I wanted to hug her and thank her for at least trying and being the only one in this fucked up family to actually show me humanity. But I knew I couldn't I could only wish.

The sight of her left me on edge. We now all sat at the table as I stared at her after 'heartfelt' greetings were exchanged. Her eyes were empty just like her sons and she wouldn't look at me. She was nonchalant. My heart broke into pieces, what did he do. She was quiet the entire dinner and eating while laughter and chatter flowed around the table. I wished I could speak to her.

"They were innocent." she suddenly said not looking at anyone in particular.

"You touched my wife." Sylas said focused on his food.

"So you decided to kill your aunts- my sisters and the sisters I made through my hard times." she said sipping her wine emotion nonexistent in her voice.

"You fucked with her, I warned you." Sylas said. Everyone else was quiet. I looked at his father who sat eating like nothing was going on. I felt like at this moment he would let them work it out. This seemed normal to everyone as Sylas' siblings minded their business.

"I grew up telling you stories about the wonders that that Asylum did for me. After your grandparents were murdered in front of me. You know how I feel about it." she chuckled biting into her food.

"And I told you I would only ask you once about the where a-bouts of my wife."

"You killed them all and you knew how much it meant to me. That was my home."

"You would be dead too if it wasn't for your darling daughter-in-law." she looked at me and then at my finger. It couldn't be. I didn't think he actually would listen to me but I guess he somehow did. I still partially believe it. This was Sylas. I remember begging for him not to harm his mother with blood all over my back. He told me I should be begging for myself but I didn't know the lengths that Sylas could go to, I needed the only person who cared enough to listen to be safe. It wasn't her fault.

"I don't allow fighting at the table. I will not speak again." His father suddenly said silence filling the room. And that's how the rest of the dinner went. This answered a lot of questions. Sylas had told me that his mother went away for sometime as a teenager before coming back to Germany to his father and becoming the best in the field. I guess it was to get help.

I almost couldn't believe that Sylas burnt it down. Almost. I didn't say a single word to her even though I wanted to, I knew it was better for everyone if I kept quiet. I held myself together and decided to be strong when congratulations were sent my way.

'Welcome to the family.' the line alone haunted me. Of course after the ring that belonged to him that would never come off my finger. I wasn't looking forward to the next dinner party we were invited to on which was in three days but I yearned to see his mother again. I wished I could comfort her in any kind of way I could.

We sat in the car on our way back home. There was a lump in my throat as my lips trembled. This was all because of me. Sylas did what he did because of me. I was tired of people I loved and people I cared for getting hurt. What was I to do though was I suppose to sit around and accept this stupid fate. That's not the woman my father raised, I might be beaten, broken and shattered but I was still my father's daughter.

I would take what Sylas would put me through if I die, I die but if I survive I will find a way, a less painful way to be free but I would find a way. I-I looked around us my heart beat picking up as the cars that were behind us were driven off the road, some of them going of in smoke and others rolling of the road. I was panicking. What was going on. I unconsciously got close to Sylas. When I looked up at him at him seeking comfort and answers, he looked down at me his eyes full of emotion I couldn't make out.

"Feeling safe yet?" he asked lightly chuckling. I couldn't believe him.

"Sylas there are cars being driven off the road and that's what's on your mind." I asked looking at him.

"Do you feel safe now?" he asked taking out his pistol and pulling me closer.

"That's not even-"

"It's a yes or no question Mäuschen." he said so easily. He looked at me if there was no world around us, it was just us.

"Yes Sylas. I feel completely safe in your arms now please do something about the gun shots. " I said sincerely looking at him as cars circled us. As he kissed me a car drove into ours almost making us swerve off the road.

"You are still in a lot of trouble Mäuschen." he said brushing my cheek before pulling me back, telling me to close my ears and sit back. I did as instructed as I watched him skilfully sending shots to the car that was currently trying to swerve us off the road. I watched from behind Sylas as he pulled the trigger and the bullet swished through the drivers head. His car rolled over and off the road crashing before catching on fire.

Sylas now seemed to be in some sort of robotic mode as he pulled out another pistol under the seat checking the bullets before opening fire at the other cars chasing us down the road. He didn't seem to be missing. Even as everything around me seemed to be in chaos as I sat so close to his arms as he shielded me from the window, I felt safe.

I seemed to be brought back into the world when the shots completely stopped and we seemed to be the only car on the road under the cover of night. I watched as he spoke German to John, the driver. He was giving him instructions, telling him to take me home. I didn't understand, it seemed like he was staying behind apparently there was another car on the way and John's life now depended on my safety on getting home. I didn't want to leave him. I knew I was a hundred percent safe with him. I was scared.

My body seemed to be going through it, before I could ask any questions a racing car came out of nowhere and before I could act I felt Sylas' body cover mine as the car clashed with our vehicle, the impact so great we were now completely off the road and continuously rolling over.

It felt so surreal as I felt his hands tighten against me, the world seemed to be spinning as the car rolled over and over and over again before I felt our bodies get thrown through the window and in the air. I couldn't feel Sylas warmth anymore I didn't understand why that caused me worry and panic. I slowly slipped out of consciousness as ringing filled my ears. I guess I wouldn't make it to that dinner after all.

Haile moved effortlessly around the kitchen as she cleaned up the mess on the floor. The paint was starting to get to her but not fully because she still found it cute. She yawned, today was her day off but she didn't seem to be getting any rest not that she was complaining. Okay maybe she was complaining a little bit.

Since early in the morning she has been dragged around and had to keep up with stories that didn't make much sense at all. She sighed at least now she was being given a little break but she could be called to duty any second so she wouldn't hold her breath. The little paint footsteps on the floor made her smile. The little artist of hers was really just living in her own world.

The rascal was taking a little nap after a lot of playing and running around. Andrea. Her daughter. Her entire world. She remembers when she found out that she was pregnant. She was surprised confused but also calm because she had once thought about the possibility. She had stopped thinking that she could predict Sylas. When she asked the doctor about her implant, the doctor had told her that there was no trace of the implant.

She was shocked. Even six feet under the man still had a part in her life. She didn't remember the implant being removed. She didn't want to think back. She didn't want to think about what Sylas did. She was so scared and confused but Andrea was the best thing that has ever happened to her. She didn't even question herself if she would keep the baby she already knew she would.

Haile was in a very bad place before her daughter. Her daughter made a lot of things clear in her life, even though her life seemed meaningless she would never take her own life that she knew. She would think about it here and there every now and then but she would never no matter. She survived Sylas so she could survive anything, that was her mantra after successfully escaping that crazy family.

Her daughter brought light and life in her life. She encouraged her to work harder for her daughters sake. Before leaving Germany she gathered some cash she had stashed away when Sylas had let her have a mini three month vacation without him, left Germany and disappeared. She made a new life and name for herself. Everything she does was for her daughter with a little help from Bella she was untraceable.

It was rough at first, after a month into her new life all she had were dreams of Sylas, not nightmares but dreams. She would wake up and find tears in her eyes. Her brain seemed to be focused on his death more than his devil of a self. In a way she doesn't believe that she truly escaped him because every time she looked at her daughter she saw him.

She remembers her heart stopping after she gave birth and had held Andrea in her arms for the first time when she opened her eyes, she was her father's daughter. Her then small blond hair which has now grown into a mane that she didn't want touched. They had to fight every time when it was time to do the braiding, or combing of her hair. Andrea also didn't like sitting still for more than five minutes which made it even more difficult.

Because of this one would think she would also hate Andrea because of her resemble to her father but Haile didn't. Something that she would never admit to anyone not even herself was that she missed a part of Sylas but she was truly happy that they were all gone. She knew couldn't just have a part of him without his other demon parts which she hated so she honestly thought it was for the best. She didn't spend a lot of time in the kitchen it made her miss Sylas and she felt low for thinking that. No more experiments, even the thought broke her heart but she was learning to live with it.

She currently resided in Egypt but she still didn't feel safe enough especially when out with her daughter, she was afraid someone would recognise them because anyone with eyes who knew Sylas could tell Andrea was Sylas' daughter, she had tried dying her daughters hair after the doctor approved but to no avail, it's not long before her blond mane turns back.

She eventually just left it like that. Plus Andrea didn't like when her mother would change her hair colour, she liked her natural hair colour because she claimed she looked like Mr Blue, her imaginary friend whom she loved. Haile at first didn't understand this whole idea with imaginary friends because she never had one but after Bella- the sweet woman who helped her with everything when she first came here and now was helping her with Andrea when she was off to work spoke to her- she eased into the idea.

She was better now than before plus Haile was in love with Mr blue because her daughter seemed to do anything she needed her to do if Mr Blue was involved, even eating veggies just because Mr Blue said they were good for her. She was grateful for her imagination. It was kind of hard restarting her life and getting used to being alone, the hardest part was severing ties with her mom.

They basically had no one in this world. Her baby had no family, just her because she would be damned if she even for a second considered Sylas' crazy part of the family as family.

She sighed looking at her now clean floor she was finally done. She gave Bella the weekend off because she would be here. As she washed her hands and put everything away she heard little footsteps rushing down into the kitchen.

"No running in the house." she said not turning around. She smiled as the footsteps stopped before walking at a fast pace.

"Mom! Mom!-" she turned around to her baby girl jumping around with a new toy she didn't recognise in her arms.

"Look what Mr Blue gave me!" she said excitingly. She smiled crouching down to her daughter. The way that her daughters eyes alone lit up made her instantly smile. She completely disregarded the fact that she didn't know of this new toy as she looked at her daughter as her mind registered everything she assumed Bella left her another toy yet again. Haile was truly grateful for Bella who had now become like family to her.

She looked at the beautiful stuffed lion. It was cute. Andrea was obsessed with lions. She couldn't stop babbling on about them ever since she watched The Lion King movie. Haile was sure she didn't understand the whole thing properly yet she was young but she seemed so engrossed and pulled in whenever she would put the movie on, so she wasn't so sure. That was the only time Andrea would sit still for more than 30 minutes. Haile has lost count of how many times they have watched that movie.

...

He looked at his family with a sense of longing in his heart as he smiled at the scene. His eyes wouldn't leave the screen even as the sound of his phone filled the air. At first he didn't understand the emotion that took over him when ever he looked at his baby. His Andrea. She was his copy and he couldn't help the pride that seemed to overtake his being every time he looked at her. He seemed to be entranced by the little thing that was always jumpy and very curious.

Sylas still didn't understand how he could love someone so much. He was willing to do anything for his daughter and Haile, his Mäuschen. He wanted to make her happy regardless of everything. Even if it meant making sacrifices and doing things he wouldn't be happy about he chose to choose silence and reason with his inner demons. They were always right but when it came to Haile and Andrea they all seemed to agree to put them first. Although it was in ways Haile wouldn't agree with but it was something.

His family was still a bit off about Haile but they wouldn't do anything. They knew he would kill them if they tried anything and as for his mother, his father got involved and he respected his father. His father came to him personally after he woke up from his coma and told him personally if the feud between him and his mother continued and if they try and hurt each other again, he would kill them.

Sylas knew his father was serious. When he woke up his mother was nowhere to be found, his father claimed he needed sometime to remind her who he is. Sylas knew if he had took the gun from his mother and put a bullet through her his father would've never rest until he killed Haile, just like he wouldn't have let his mother live if anything would have happened to his wife. Yes he was his son but at the end of the day, it was his mother that they were talking about.

They were alike like that and for the sake of Haile and his unborn baby he chose Haile. For the first time in his life he chose her and he was happy with his decision.

He couldn't have risked anything happening to his wife. His father didn't understand his strategy neither was he happy about it even though he was obsessed with his grandchild. Sylas shook his head, Haile was very inattentive. Andrea already met her grandpa many times. He has never seen his father laugh so much. She called him 'pow pow' and for now he was okay with her calling him Mr Blue, he didn't want to freak out his wife.

Sylas was glad his daughter loved his gift. He couldn't wait for Haile to go to work so he could go and spend time with his daughter. Jolene known to Halle as Bella one of his body guards and one of the best, she was sent by Sylas to look after his family so it wouldn't be a problem. Before Sylas came back to Germany with Haile after his mother helped her flee the country he had set a plan out for her disappearance because he knew his mother.

Jolene was in charge of that plan, the only person aside himself that has known and helped Haile with her every move was Jolene, not a single member of his family had that information. While in a coma the only thing that had gone though Sylas' mind was his wife. When he woke up, he had to remind himself everyday that he swore to himself to do better and make her happy.

His father wanted him to take her, that was also what Sylas wanted, he thought about it every single day but he couldn't. He wanted to be human enough for Haile so as she calls it. Sylas tried psychologists but they didn't seem to understand that Haile was his very breath. They annoyed him insinuating he was crazy of course he knew that, that wasn't the problem. He wasn't paying them to tell him what he already knew, he was paying them to fix him for his wife so she could be happy with him.

They failed. For the first time in his life he had chose to wait even though he had the power to take Haile. It was very hard and his patience was running out but looking at them had motivated him and made him close to snapping at the same time. His child was now 2 years and six months, Sylas himself sometimes couldn't understand how he was still not with them. At first he thought he was fighting a losing battle but now he knew for sure. It wasn't until yesterday that everything was finally clear to him.

Yesterday marked the 24th psychologist he has been to that failed. His mind was spiralling and he almost set his course to home and home was where Haile and his daughter was. He had needed motivation. That's why he was in this room staring at his family through the screen, just like yesterday but the difference about today was that he now had some clarity. He really wanted to get better for Haile and by better he needed to be sure of himself that he wouldn't kill her one day and he didn't want to be the cause of her tears.

In fact he wanted to plant her a garden of corpses of anyone who would dare make her sad. Not just anyone would understand but he understood, but he didn't think she would like that. The fact that he now thought deeply about it meant progress, but that's not from the psychologists that's from the time he had with himself in that coma his mother had put him in, Eight months is a very long time, when he woke up the gym became his only therapy session. The psychologists have failed and he himself has lost reason. He needed his family here.

He watched her pick up their baby walking around the house with her little pyjamas mocking him. He clenched his jaw controlling his breath. It was like Haile was deliberately making things hard for him. Sylas has missed her, he was even considering overlooking the fact that she threw his ring away at the first chance she got. Sylas was still Sylas at the end of the day the difference now was that he was willing to be more for her but for now she would have to deal with him.

Sylas swore to himself that he would deal with everything differently and he would try to be more understanding but one thing he would not and would never understand, was Haile's insinuation of any form of leaving him. He knew he would never accept that. He wanted to do better for her because she belonged to him and him alone.

Sylas thought surely Haile would see he has changed, he won't address the fact that she left even though he knew she needed to, it still evoked something in him. To himself that was progress. He was originally going to put her in a wheelchair for choosing his mother and letting her hide her but not anymore. He decided to let bygones be bygones, even with all that flowing through his mind he still didn't understand why she threw away his ring.

A smile made it's way to his face as his pilot announced their arrival in Egypt. Sylas softly shut his laptop and stood up ready to leave his jet. He had questions for his Mäuschen that needed answers. Aside everything, the conclusion he came up with last night was the only thing that made him see reason. Of course he should have known. No one would make him better for Haile, only Haile had the power to do that.

His only mission now was to let his wife guide him to being the man she wants him to be. He knew it would take time and she wouldn't leave without a fight but time was up and he wouldn't exactly be asking. He could only wait so long. He tried but everything failed him. As he got closer to her he could feel himself spiralling, it would take time but he was willing to take that time but only with Haile. It was time to get his family back.

...

•The End•

200

Made in United States
Troutdale, OR
02/29/2024